Marta Gets Soapy

Book Five of the Housekeeping Detective Series

Cyndia Rios-Myers

This book is dedicated to my wonderful son. My wonderful boy: you are almost done with high school. You are almost an adult. Staying at home with you and being with you every single day is the best single thing I have ever done. I am so proud of you and could not love you any more than I do. Mommy loves you.

Acknowledgements

Marta's been on the back burner for a minute now. It's been maybe two years since I published *Marta Gets the Ax*, which is book four of the series.

Marta has continued to be alive in the back of my brain. The usual folks keep asking me about book five: my big sister Rachel, my mother Cristina, and Becky and Caroline and so many other good people. What got me to commit Marta's latest adventure to paper was the simple desire to finish something I started.

Okay; a bonus desire is the dream to see the Housekeeping Detective Series as a TV series…on TV. There are so many great mystery shows on TV now. So much work appears to go into one-hour episodes of a good whodunit show. I hope Marta makes it to the small screen.

Biggest thanks go to my son and to my husband Colby. And the readers! Thank you for reading!

A Note to my Readers

For my gentle readers – whom I love – there is profanity in this book. While in my day-to-day life I choose not to speak in profane words, a lot of other people do. Some of the more colorful characters in this book series speak using profane words, too. Even Marta slips and drops an f-bomb here or there.

Also, this is a work of fiction. I made all of it up. If any aspects of this story appear to mirror real-life events, it is all a coincidence.

Also, this is my work. Don't try to steal it. You don't have permission to do that.

Thanks for reading!

Table of Contents

Chapter One

I felt guilty. I was speeding home in crazy Chicago traffic knowing that my relationship with a police officer would get me out of a citation. I'd yet to test that particular perk that came with being the serious girlfriend of Detective Kevin Connelly.

Tonight, though, I had to push it.

I did not have a date with my boyfriend, nor did I have a private investigation to conduct.

No; the matter at hand was hurrying home so that I could watch *¿Quién ama a Ana Luz*? – a Spanish-language Puerto Rican soap opera with my mother - over the phone.

"Oh my gosh," I groaned as I drove through a yellow light that was clearly turning red. "What are you doing, Marta?"

Of late, I had planned my daily schedule down to the half-hour. Kevin had not yet noticed, but over the past month, our dates and meetups only happened after 7:30 p.m. My favorite telenovela came on weekdays at six p.m., Central Standard Time. In Puerto Rico, it aired at seven p.m. Atlantic Standard Time. My mother (who lived in Puerto Rico) and I spoke on speakerphone (on my sleuther phone, so Kevin's calls and texts wouldn't interrupt my chat time with my mom) while we watched the one-hour show.

At 6:01 p.m., I huffed and puffed as I charged into my apartment. Quickly (and after closing and latching my front door), I turned the TV on and called my mom.

"¡Estas tarde!" My mom complained.

"It's not my fault!" I said as I kicked my shoes off and sank onto my couch. "Barney got a new carpet installed in his haberdashery last night - without telling me! The installers put all of his clothing racks back right, but they didn't tell him how much the carpet would shed! I had to vacuum the carpet four times! And it was still shedding!"

"That sounds like a business problem."

"Mom, Barney's one of my clients. He's my landlord, too, now," I said as I waved at the apartment around me. "Also, he's kind of a friend. I can't allow Barney to lose face while millionaire and sometimes billionaire customers come into his store to peruse his wares."

"I don't know what those last three words mean."

"Mom," I grunted. "You understand the sentiment. I can't let him look bad."

"*Aha, aha. Cállate que va a comenzar el show.*"

Zoraida Mercado - my mom - was rude, but she was right. I needed to shut up because the show was about to start.

"This show is amazing!" My mother said. Apparently, I had to shut up but she did not. Still, I didn't interrupt her.

"This is not typical!" Mom continued. "A *telenovela* where the protagonist is not going to end up with the man she loves! I am surprised the television network allowed it."

"Well, it is only going to air for about a month," was my qualification.

"Aha. They had a break between two other longer *telenovelas*, so they let this show through," Mom said. "Okay! Let's be quiet now. It's about to start!"

"Fine, Mom," I said as I settled into my couch.

"Okay! But don't hit pause! I don't have cable you can pause and I am not going to wait for you!"

I listened to my mother's warning but would pause the show if I needed to. Because I was a grown-up like that.

The show opened up with the protagonist - Ana Luz - catching her love interest - Ángel Alexis Garcés - chatting up Ana Luz's best friend Marielena. Ana Luz was standing by the entrance of the *cafetería* where Marielena worked but was not making her presence known as she wanted to snoop in on her love interest speaking to her best friend.

"Ana Luz is trying to surprise her best friend Marielena with donuts and coffee!" My mom said, stating the obvious. "What is Ángel Alexis doing there?!"

The shadiness occurring between Ana Luz's best friend Marielena and Ana Luz's romantic interest – Ángel Alexis - was not the only problem, though.

"I know why Ana Luz and Ángel Alexis don't end up together," I said to my mother.

"Why?!"

"Things are not going to work out between Ana Luz and Ángel Alexis because Ana Luz is stupid."

"Don't say that!"

My mother was very protective of the novela's protagonist.

"Why is Ana Luz taking coffee and donuts to a woman who works at a coffee shop?"

"*Ave Maria*," my mom said. "You are right."

My non-sleuther/personal phone rang. I looked at the screen to see if it was Kevin. It was not, so I ignored the call. I went back to watching Ana Luz cry; from a corner, the protagonist watched her best friend laugh and touch Ángel Alexis' big bicep.

Then my phone rang again. Sighing, I picked it up.

"Can you call me back later? I'm in the middle of something," I said to the annoying caller.

"No, you are not. You are going to take my call now because Wanda got me sucked into this stupid telenovela," Rafael Morales said.

Rafy - my brother - was a police detective who, like my parents, lived in Arecibo, Puerto Rico. While I wanted to take the time to insult him for lowering his standards and watching a telenovela, I didn't have the time.

"Fine. Shut up and I am going to put you on speaker."

So, I did.

"I don't understand why you talk to your brother like that," Mom complained.

"I don't either," Rafy said.

"Shut up, Momma's boy," I barked.

"Yes. *Cállate*," Mom said to her son. "We only talk about the show."

"Fine," Rafy grumbled. "I'll talk about the show. Ana Luz is stupid. That's why Ángel Alexis can't date her."

"That's what I said!" I exclaimed.

"Marielena works at a coffee shop! She probably hates coffee!" He continued. "Why is that blockhead bringing her friend coffee?"

"*Tienes razón*," Mom added.

"Also, Marielena has a banging booty. Ana Luz has the prettier face, but, she's kind of flat."

"You are so gross!" I yelled at my brother.

"¡Ave Maria!" complained my mother.

"Just saying," Rafy added.

I grunted and rolled my eyes, but kept watching the show. Ana Luz never left her secret spot but watched her best friend and her love interest flirt with each other.

"You know, sometimes you have to let men go," I said to my mother.

"You can do that in the United States," Mom said. "But not here in Puerto Rico. There are not enough men to go around. If you find a halfway decent man, you have to get him and fight to keep him."

I grunted in disgust. "I hate that you're right."

"More females than males here in PR. It's a sad fact," Rafy said.

But he didn't sound sad.

“There’s quantity and then there’s quality,” I replied.

“More of a reason to fight for a good man!” Mom explained.

“How is Ángel Alexis is a good man if he’s flirting with the best friend of the girl he’s thinking about dating?” I argued.

“*Bueno*. I said he was a *halfway* decent man. Not fully good,” Mom qualified.

“She did say that,” Rafy interjected.

“Then what do women do about a Puerto Rican man who is fully good?” I asked.

“They lock that up in high school, just like Wanda did to me,” said Rafy.

I rolled my eyes. “Where is your wife?”

“Driving the boys home from an out-of-town baseball game. I couldn’t make it because I was working late.”

My nephews - Julián and José - were teenaged twin boys who played for their junior high baseball team. They were very good baseball players.

“Oh, man,” I said to Rafy. “It sucks that you missed that game.”

Rafy groaned. “I know. But...shit’s going down here. I couldn’t leave.”

“Hey! We only talk about the *novela* now!” Mom barked.

I was quiet, but all the while wondering what was going down at Rafy's precinct. Rafy - like my boyfriend - was a police detective.

Once upon a time, I'd been a police officer myself. That was many moons ago, though. These days, I use my sleuthing skills to do good housekeeping for my cleaning clients. I also did under-the-table detective work for select clients. I was very good at both occupations.

I believed that my best skill was the ability to focus on the information that was present on the scene, as well as identifying absent information.

Ana Luz - the telenovela protagonist - was a mystery herself. While she could not use rational thought in gift ideas for her best friend, she was pretty savvy with context clues when it came to people. In a later scene of the episode, I watched Ana Luz as she politely tried to suss out what Ángel Alexis had been doing earlier that morning (chilling with Ana Luz's best friend). Ana Luz caught Ángel Alexis in a lie but did not call him on it.

"I wonder if she's an idiot savant," I mused out loud. "Maybe she's good at reading people."

"Don't call her an idiot," Mom defended.

"She didn't," Rafy interjected. "That's not what idiot savant means."

"An idiot savant is a mentally challenged person who is gifted in one small area, but ignorant of others," Esteban Morales called out over the phone line my mother was supposed to be alone on.

"I didn't know Dad was on speaker, too," I accused.

"Yeah," Rafy unhappily chimed in.

"He is," Mom said.

"Ana Luz, while being an idiot, is not an idiot savant," Dad said in a droll tone.

"Don't talk about her like that!" said Zoraida.

"But she is amusing," Dad added. "I see what you mean about the writing, Marta," Dad said to me. "The writers of this show took a risk with this. So did the producers and the network for that matter."

I said nothing to my father's praise, as I was still in a sore place with him due to a big lie I'd caught him in. We'd recently begun talking again, but it was rough going.

"I enjoy it," I finally said.

"Yeah," Rafy chimed in. "Look at Ana Luz. She is...accepting what is. Ángel Alexis is interested in another woman. Ana Luz is accepting that - and herself."

"Ana Luz needs to get with the program!" Mom exclaimed. "If she lets Ángel Alexis get distracted, she is going to lose him and she is going to be a *jamona*!"

The word '*jamona*' meant a woman who could not find a husband. The connotation was very negative.

"Unless Ana Luz is playing another game," Dad said.

Instantly, he'd grabbed my attention.

"How so?" asked my brother.

"Ana Luz is being intelligent and mysterious, which is attractive. Ángel Alexis doesn't see that now, but he will. Maybe when he's dating Marielena. Perhaps Ana Luz's motivation is that she wants Ángel Alexis to get this Marielena business out of her system. Maybe Ana Luz is testing her best friend, too. Maybe Ana Luz is fooling all of us - the viewers. Maybe she doesn't want Ángel Alexis at all."

Of course, my dad, the former FBI agent, would see clues we'd missed. I would have caught them, too, but not as quickly as he did.

"You are good with mystery," Rafy said.

"How many times do I have to apologize for that old shit?" Dad angrily inquired.

My brother and I - me a former police officer and Rafy a current one - did not have a problem with dad's "old shit" - his past as a federal agent. What we had a problem with was the fact that he hid it from us. I'd only discovered it when another federal agent had shared that bit of information with me.

"You are not going to apologize for that again," Mom said, presumably to my father.

I sighed. "How about we talk about Ana Luz and wonder why she isn't calling out her best friend?"

The current scene was dinner at Ana Luz's parents' house, where both Ana Luz and Marielena were present.

"That's easy," Rafy said. "Friends are harder to break up with than boyfriends and girlfriends."

"True story," I said in answer.

The episode concluded with Ana Luz sweeping sand off of her beachside condo's back patio. Ana Luz retrieved a ringing cell phone from her apron pocket.

"Who wears an apron anymore?" Rafy scoffed.

"Shut up!" Mom said.

I agreed with Mom's sentiment. The novela's scene was laced with meanings and subtexts that I did not want to miss.

Ana Luz looked at the cell phone screen and saw that it was Ángel Alexis who was calling her. She let it ring four times before rejecting the call and putting the phone back in her pocket.

Ana Luz grabbed the broom again and carried on with sweeping the back porch. When she was done, she leaned on a wall and smiled.

"I don't get why she's smiling," Rafy said.

"Because she is realizing what it is she can control - her surroundings," I explained.

"But it's a half-smile," Mom added. "She isn't completely happy."

"She knows who she can trust," Rafy said.

I shrugged. "Well. Not exactly. I think she knows the most important thing, though," I said.

"What?" asked Mom.

"That it doesn't matter how long or how well you know someone. You can never guarantee the behavior of another person," I answered.

My somber statement coincided with the end of the TV show, as well as the conversations with my brother and even my father. I was going to hang up with my mom when she spoke up.

"You are off speaker now and I am on the *marquesina*."

I didn't know why she wanted to tell me that she was on the porch, but whatever.

"Okay. What's going on?"

"Your father. You need to talk to him more."

Mom's angry whisper revealed her frustration.

"I am talking to him, Mom," I angrily said. "I talked to him yesterday!"

"No. Not like you used to."

"That's going to take a while, Mom. But I'm working on it."

"Your father is getting older. Your conversations with him matter to him a lot. Get past your anger and be a good daughter."

I sighed and wondered if I would have been as good at guilting my adult child as my mom was with me.

"Mom? I got to go. I have to call Kevin."

"Okay. Think about what I said."

I grunted, gave her my love, and then hung up. I stared at my phone for a bit, wondering if I should call my father.

I called my boyfriend instead.

"Hey, you," Kevin said to me.

I could hear phones ringing and conversations going on in the police precinct, which was where he was.

"Hey, you. How's your afternoon and evening been?" I asked him.

"Busy, of course."

Kevin had been a criminal investigator for a few years, which was how we'd met. However, a few of the higher-ups wanted Kevin to get into the homicide detective business. I wasn't a fan, and neither was he.

"Can I bore you with details of my day?" I asked.

"I'd love nothing better. How about this? I'll be there in five."

I beamed. "Can you make it fifteen? Get us donuts or something to eat? I have to shower still."

"You haven't showered yet? How long have you been home?"

I blushed as I thought about the *novela* I'd been watching.

"Not as long as I'd like. Barney had a new carpet installed last night. It's been fuzzing like crazy."

"Huh. How long do new carpets shed for again?"

I hummed as I thought of the answer. "It can take months sometimes. It all depends on the quality and how much the carpet is vacuumed."

Kevin was quiet for a moment. I smiled, as I knew what he was doing. He was saving my bit of housekeeping knowledge into his mental logbook of facts.

"Alright. But we'll do Chinese instead."

"Yay," I excitedly said.

"I'll let myself in," Kevin added.

I let out a slow breath, as I needed to calm my body down. I'd given Kevin a key to my new apartment, as he was my local emergency person. Also, we were getting closer and closer to becoming completely intimate. The hang-ups to sexual relations were my re-found devotion to my faith and the fact that I did not yet have an engagement ring on my left ring finger.

The passion, however, was there.

Kevin laughed. "I'll be there in a bit."

"Okay. Drive safe."

Sixteen minutes later held us at my kitchen dining table eating Chinese for dinner. My new apartment was five minutes away from Kevin's precinct. I was a fan of that, as was Kevin.

"Doña Justa called me today," I said as I sighed.

Kevin set his fork down and looked at me.

"Really?"

I nodded. "Yeah."

"What did Doña Justa say? Did she want you to move back into your old place?"

Doña Justa was the landlady of the previous apartment I'd lived in. I'd lived in the third-floor apartment of her brownstone home for nearly fifteen years. However, life changes - on my part (my young grandson and my boyfriend) were not things Doña Justa was a fan of. I was ready to move out and move on, so I did.

"Basically. Doña Justa's new tenants have been horrible. She smartened up, though, and only does month-to-month leases until she gets to know the new tenants. She told me that she would allow me to come back - and at my previous rental rate. I wished her the best, but told her that I was happy where I was."

Kevin's beautiful blue eyes seared into me. "I bet she wasn't a fan of that."

I laughed. "She kind of hung up on me."

Kevin laughed and patted my hand.

After eating our meals, we moved to the living room couch and watched TV.

"I'm glad you are happy here at your new place," Kevin said.

"Me too."

"It's not supposed to be permanent, though," he added.

Kevin wasn't wrong. What was supposed to be permanent was my buying a home. A few months past, I'd found the house of my dreams. That had fallen through, though, as my realtor had been less than diligent in answering her voicemail messages. The other permanent thing was supposed to be a ring on my finger. Well over a year ago, my boyfriend had told me that we would be "serious" in less than a year.

I was still waiting.

Instead of giving Kevin a hard time, I said something else.

"What is permanence? At best, it's nothing but a promise."

Kevin turned to face me. "That's a somber statement."

"Maybe."

I tried to lighten the mood by cuddling into his side. After a brief pause, he pulled me close. He was quiet for the rest of the time he spent with me. That was okay, as I had my own things to mull over, too.

Chapter Two

That night's dreams featuring worrying scenes regarding my future with Kevin. My father factored in there, too. In dreams, he told me that a good daughter learns from her father - willing or not.

Even though he was a dream version of my dad, I still thought his words were probably cryptic garbage he'd learned at Quantico – the training academy for the FBI.

"Can't trust a fed," I said as I got out of bed in the morning.

My mood wasn't good. However, a phone call from Awilda, a friend I'd helped with a haunted house almost one year passed, was very welcome.

"Hey, lady! How are you?" I asked as I drove to my first cleaning job of the day. "How are the kids and Arturo and the acting going?"

Awilda laughed out loud. "Give me a minute - that's a lot to unpack and share. Well, Arturo made Master Chief - E9 - the most senior enlisted rank in the Navy. That fucker is trying to sell me on reenlisting."

Yikes. Awilda was not pulling the punches as far as her sailor husband's career was concerned. She hated it.

One year ago, Awilda's aunt had hired me to help find out who was dropping off witchy items at her niece's house. At that time, I'd learned that Awilda was having trouble in her marriage due to her husband's military career. Awilda wanted to be done with the Navy, while her husband did not.

"So much shit went down!" she continued. "I showed Arturo the two-thousand-dollar Expedia gift card I bought for myself. But I suspected that he was going to call my bluff," she said with a sigh. "So, I did it, Marta. I went and did it."

"Oh, my goodness. Hold on! I'm too far for coffee and crackers, but I am going to stop at this Krispy Kreme drive-thru for donuts and coffee. Hold on! Don't say anything else!"

My first cleaning job of the day would have to wait.

Awilda laughed. "Go ahead. The kids are at school right now and I'm here drinking my coffee."

Coffee and crackers were the typical snacks I liked to indulge in while gabbing. Ten minutes later I parked outside of the Krispy Kreme with a hot glazed donut in one hand and a hotter coffee in the other.

"Okay. I'm ready."

"I did it, Marta. I bought three one-way tickets to Puerto Rico for me and the kids. We leave this weekend."

My mouth dropped open. I bit into a donut while I tried to find words to express my shock.

"No kidding?"

"No. I can't keep threatening Arturo and not delivering. He went so far as to get travel guides for the three places we could be stationed next."

"Oh, wow. How are Chayanne and Dagmar with the whole thing?" Awilda's kids – her daughter Dagmar in particular – had played a role in bringing peace to Awilda and Arturo's witchy home. Her son Chayanne had sweetly supported his sister Dagmar, too.

Awilda sighed. "They feel torn. They will miss their dad, but they miss their family in Puerto Rico, too. My parents are getting older."

"What did Arturo say?"

"He's in shock. I am, too."

"Where will you go? What will you do?"

"My brother is going to let me live in his town apartment rent-free while I get something else going. I know someone who works at a bank. They are looking for bilingual tellers. It is crap pay to start, but I think there's growth potential."

I sipped my coffee. "Wow. You thought this through. You have an actual plan."

"I do. But shit; that's not why I'm calling!" Awilda said with a smile in her voice.

I laughed. "Okay. I am all ears."

"Look. I got a referral for you. It's kind of weird, but the work should be down there in Chicago. It seems like it would be easy."

I set my coffee cup down in my console's cupholder.

"A referral, huh? Tell me about it."

"A girl I know, well - she's not a girl anymore - she's twenty-four, but acts like a girl sometimes."

I laughed. "I know the type."

"I knew her through her mom. Her mom – God rest her soul – worked at the Puerto Rican restaurant I get my *pasteles* and my *guineos en escabeche* from."

The thought of the traditional Puerto Rican food dishes had my mouth watering.

"Oh, wow. Are the bananas they use for the *guineos en escabeche* any good? Because those are hard to get right."

"Yeah, right? I think it's all about the *mollejas*. If they can't get the *mollejas* right, they don't need to mess around with the recipe," Awilda said.

I laughed. "I don't like the *mollejas*. Do you know that they are gizzards?"

Awilda laughed. "I do!"

"We'll have to save the gizzard debate for later. Tell me more about this friend of yours."

"Amanda Trujillo. And calling her a friend might be a bit of a stretch. You'll understand once I tell you more."

Fifteen minutes later held me apprised of the potential case.

"Okay, Awilda. This gig sounds weird, but it is also interesting and maybe kind of distracting. I need a bit of a distraction now, too."

"Don't we all," Awilda sighed. "Should I tell Amanda to call you?"

"Give her my sleuther phone number. But, first, tell her that the non-refundable deposit for this case will be five hundred dollars. It's a fair amount, and it might make her second guess this hunt of hers."

"I'll tell her. Shit. I have got to go now. My brother's calling me - probably about his house."

"Wow. That's real."

"All I have time for is real, Marta. I ain't got time for maybes or perhaps."

I let out a breath. "True story."

After disconnecting with Awilda, I headed to Jane Knight's condo – my first cleaning gig of the day. I dashed out of my car, hoping that Jane was gone and would be unaware of the fact that I would have been late.

"Thank God," I said as I walked into her empty kitchen.

"You're late!" I heard. Oddly, the barking voice had come from the ceiling.

"Did you install a security system?"

"Yes. With cameras and a clock. You are late."

I sighed and nodded. "I know. I'm sorry. I had a weird night and an interesting morning."

"Spill. Make it juicy enough, and I'll forget your failure in adhering to the schedule."

I took my jacket off and set it on one of her barstools.

"You should hear how your voice sounds. It bounces off the walls and sounds...scary and threatening."

Jane giggled. "Does it?"

"It does!"

"Score! Now. Spill."

I shrugged. "Well, the first thing bothering me won't be news to you. Kevin said we'd be serious in a year. Yet here's my left hand - devoid of an engagement ring."

I held up my left hand to the camera.

"No need to hold your hand up. This camera has thousands of megapixels."

My brow furrowed. "Aren't there like...a million pixels in a megapixel?"

"Don't talk down to me about my quantification methods."

"I'm just trying to do the math. It doesn't make sense to count a larger number into a smaller one."

"You've reported the first thing, which I will address in a moment. Let's hear the rest."

Darn. I had been hoping to distract Jane from her train of thought. Well, she wasn't a defense attorney for nothing.

"Okay. Secondly, things are still weird with my dad. Thirdly, I might have a new case."

"Ah. Very interesting things. On your first item: one year to a woman is not always one year to a man. He's probably going to propose, but he's probably busy with work stuff."

"If I was a twenty or thirty-something-year-old woman, I would allow that. However, I am not that. I am a forty-something-year-old woman with a rapidly approaching best-buy date. You know where I am coming from."

"Ouch! I'm not forty yet."

"But your egg timer is ticking loudly. You said that yourself."

Jane groaned. "I know. The investment banker guy told me that he didn't want any more kids, so we're done."

"Did you want to make babies with him?"

"I didn't even want to *sleep* with him," Jane added.

"Fair enough."

"As far as the other stuff is concerned, parents are hard, too. But, if you are lucky, they aren't going anywhere - for a while. Your dad will understand. As far as your potential case is concerned, I am going to want details on that, but not right now."

I sighed as I looked up at the camera again. "I'm sorry I'm late. Want me to put something in your crockpot for you?"

"I forgot to take meat out," Jane said with a sigh.

"I'll find something I can throw in for you."

"That will work. Gotta go."

"Alright."

Jane - my housekeeping client, sometimes attorney, and friend was someone I knew well, though.

"It smells like mildew in here," I said to the ceiling-mounted camera.

"What?" Jane loudly exclaimed.

I laughed and shook my head. "It doesn't. I was just testing to see if you were still watching."

"You suck."

I shrugged. I then waved at the camera and carried on with my cleaning. After leaving beef stew (using meat I'd defrosted in the microwave) in a crock pot, I headed out.

The rest of the day held predictable work, fortunately. I cleaned for my residential clients as well as my business ones before heading home.

At the last moment, I did a detour and pointed my car to the place of business of my friend Angie Bonacci – aka Indigo Cassiopeia.

"Hey. I thought you were Catholic," my friend said to me.

I laughed as I entered the Wicca store. "I'm merely here to convert you to the faith."

Angie laughed out loud. "I think you mean to revert me. I'm about to close for the day. Let me lock up. We can have tea and gab."

"Sounds good."

After some Earl Grey and crackers, I told Angie what was bothering me.

"Am I the oldest of your friends?"

I shook my head. "No. My oldest friend is a widowed nun."

"Aren't they all? Being that nuns are married to Jesus and all."

I set my teacup down and pondered Angie's question. "That's a good question. I am going to have to think about that."

Angie laughed and waved me off. "Okay. Here's what I think. Kevin's about...two months late with an engagement ring?"

"Yes," I said as I blushed.

"And you are worried that he won't propose and you'll have to wait and get older."

"Yes, and ouch."

Angie ignored that. "You have to give credit to his occupation. Being a Chicago police detective is the most dangerous job he could be doing. His concept of timing is probably different than yours."

"And I will give an allowance for that. But how much?"

"I think you'll know when. I don't think that time is now, but when it comes, you'll know."

I looked at my teacup and then at my friend.

"Did you just read my tea leaves?"

Angie laughed out loud and hard. "I knew you were going to say that!"

"I couldn't help myself," I said as I laughed, too.

"Look; I am proud of you for being real about where you are in life. I'm here for you - no matter what. However, I have some busy shit coming."

"Really? What?"

Angie beamed - making her look so pretty. "I am two weeks into foster parent training."

My mouth dropped open. "What?"

"Yeah. My eggs went bad, but I am going to be a mom anyway. I am going to foster Charity Russo. I am going to adopt her."

Excitement and elation filled me. "Oh, my goodness! Come here! That's worth a hug!"

Angie gave me a quick hug. "Yeah. So... I won't be too available here for a few more weeks. I've got training and classes every night. I'm trying to expedite my classes and background checks so that Charity doesn't have to remain in her current foster care home much longer."

"God rest Greta's soul," I whispered.

"Amen," Angie echoed - and with much ardor.

Greta Russo had been my most recent sleuthing case. Greta – a woman dying of cancer – was her granddaughter Charity's sole caregiver. Greta wanted me to find her party-loving daughter Cassidy. Greta wanted Cassidy to grow up and owe up to her responsibilities – that of being a mother to Charity.

I found Cassidy, but, sadly, learned that Cassidy was not ready to change her situation.

One month ago, Greta Russo succumbed to cancer. Her granddaughter went to foster care. But hopefully, Charity would be rescued by Angie - the Russo family friend who'd referred me to Greta in the first place.

"Yeah. I am going to do right by Charity," Angie said as she walked me to the door. "And Charity is going to give me something I've wanted for so long - motherhood."

I laughed and hugged my friend again. "That's so wonderful."

"Thank you, friend. And I don't mean to chase you out the door, but I have to get to the community college for class."

"Then I'll leave. Call me when you get a break?"

"Will do," Angie said as she closed the door behind me.

Once home, I showered and got ready to watch the *novela* with my mom. During a commercial break, I stated the obvious.

"It looks like it's just you and me, tonight, Ma."

"*Sí*. Julián and José have a game. Both Wanda and Rafy are working late, so your father is taking them to their game."

I smiled. "That's so good of him."

"Your father is a good man," Mom answered.

I sighed.

"Okay. The show's back on. No talking." Mom said.

That worked for me. Sometimes people talked and talked, but nothing got said.

Chapter Three

Amanda Trujillo – Awilda's sleuthing referral – called me bright and early the next day.

"Hi! This is Amanda. Is this Marta? Awilda told me about you. Am I calling you too early?"

I chuckled in response – trying to make my nervous caller a bit more comfortable. "No. Seven a.m. is fine. I've been up for a bit and have about half an hour until I need to get to my first job for the day."

"Oh. What is it you do full-time?"

"I'm a housekeeper. I own my own business."

"Oh, wow! What a coincidence! My aunt is a housekeeper, too. The pay isn't great, but she gets good holiday bonuses. Do your clients give you bonuses?"

Amanda Trujillo was a nervous talker. Thinking quickly, I got up from my kitchen table and reached for my recorder, pad, and pen. I hit the record button before answering Amanda.

"I don't want to bore you with my housekeeping business stuff, Amanda. Awilda told me that you might have a case for me. Is that right?"

Amanda let out a shuddering breath. "Yeah, that's right. I... have a case for you?"

"Do you want to tell me more about it?"

"Umm. Can we meet instead? It's private stuff that I'm not entirely proud of. But maybe if you can see me face-to-face, you'll know that I am a good person. I'm just desperate."

I looked at my wall calendar and did some quick thinking.

"Are you in Chicago?"

"I'm in Wisconsin, but I live near the border. Are you familiar with the Pilsen neighborhood? I know people down by there. I can meet you there this evening."

That was right by my neighborhood.

"Okay. I can meet you at five p.m. But no later than that. Is there a Panera out there or something like that?" I asked.

I knew the answer, though. There were two Panera breads within walking distance of my studio apartment. Andrea Trujillo didn't need to know that, though.

"No! There's a place called Cookie's! It's on Sebastian Avenue. They have the best croissants there."

I'd not yet been there, but I'd seen the locale.

"Okay. I will meet you at five o'clock this evening. How will you be dressed?"

"Oh! I'll have a gray sweater with black tassels on it. I have long, dark hair, too. You won't miss me."

"Alright. I'll see you at five."

That morning and afternoon I rushed through my cleaning jobs - although I did them thoroughly. The prospect of working another sleuther case was exciting.

Over my last phone call to Awilda, she'd had given me the weird, but bare bones of the case. There was a lot I did not understand. I looked forward to getting the answers from Amanda – my potential client.

At five o'clock on the dot, I walked into Cookie's. Amanda was right about the quality of the pastries; Cookie's air smelled of rising yeast and other wonderful things.

I stared at the cafe's offerings - beautiful, crusty-looking bread rolls lying in wait on trays within a large glass case. I was in trouble.

A second later, I caught sight of someone waving at me. Seated at a booth was a young woman wearing a tasseled sweater.

I blushed and nervously smiled as I approached her table.

"Marta?" she asked of me.

I nodded. "Yeah. How did you know it was me?"

"You look Puerto Rican."

I gave a slow nod, as her assessment had been a fair one. I stared at Amanda, noting darker skin, but sharp features. Silently, I wondered what she was.

"Oh! I'm half black and half Dominican. My mom's black. Please - sit down."

Invited, I did as requested.

"Did you want to get something to drink?" Amanda asked.

Without waiting for an answer, Amanda waved at someone. A smiling waitress came to our table.

"Hi. Can you get my friend a classic croissant and a coffee?"

"Sugar and milk?" inquired the waitress.

"Both. Thank you," was my answer.

Five minutes later held me eating a delectable croissant.

"Wow," I said between bites.

Amanda laughed. "This place is great!"

"For sure."

After finishing my treat and having a few sips of coffee, I produced a pad and my recorder.

"Wow. That looks so professional," Amanda marveled.

"I haven't hit record yet, nor have I started jotting anything down. We are both at the 'walk away' moment of this job."

"I understand," Amanda said, sitting a bit straighter in her booth seat.

"Did Awilda tell you how much I charge?"

Andrea sighed. "Yeah. Five hundred," she whispered to me.

I nodded. "Yeah. It's a non-refundable deposit."

"Why is it so much? It's not like you have to drive to Great Lakes. Awilda told me you had to do that for her."

The truth was that I cited a figure of five hundred dollars because I kind of wanted to scare Amanda away. The more

I considered what Awilda told me of the case, the less I liked it.

"I am my own boss. I can set my own rates. I want to hear your story from you. Depending on what I hear, I might be persuaded to take your case. I might be flexible on the cost, too."

"Okay. That's good news."

"From this moment forward, I'm recording things. I'll probably jot down notes, too."

Amanda reached for a hank of her dark hair and ran her fingers through it. She was nervous, which was a good sign. It meant that she had not rehearsed what she was going to say.

"Okay. Um. Where do I start?"

"What do you want me to do for you, Amanda?"

"I want you to find my father for me."

A very reasonable request.

"Why?"

"Why what?"

"Why do you want me to find your father?"

"Uh," she said as she dramatically rolled her eyes. "He's like my dad. I have a right to know where he is and why he doesn't want to be a part of my life."

In Spanish, I wrote the word '*afectada*,' which translated to 'affected.' Amanda Trujillo was performing.

"I want something real, Amanda. I don't care that your dad isn't with you. I want to know why you want to pay me to find him."

Amanda put her hand down and took a breath. "Okay. Yeah. I... I listened to my mom; you know? My dad bailed out on my mom, me, and my sister when we were like six and four years of age. Mom was always sure that Dad would come back."

I heard a hitch in her voice. I recalled Awilda telling me that Amanda's mother had passed away.

"But he didn't! He never even paid child support! I mean, I knew he was alive because I had some family friends tell me that he was shacking up with other women and stuff."

Amanda took another sip of her coffee, appearing to try to calm her nerves.

"You seem angry, but not bitter. That's impressive," I said to Amanda.

Amanda chuckled and rolled her eyes. "That's owed to my mom. She made me and my younger sister pretend like Dad was still around. I know that's weird. Mom wanted us to not act like we were brokenhearted because he was gone. That meant doing chores at home, getting good grades at school, getting jobs, going to college, and graduating. I did that, by the way. Two years ago. I work with computers and make good money. My sister is pre-med."

"Again, I'm impressed."

"Yeah, so is everyone else," she added, but didn't sound sharp as she said it. "I thought that if I did well - that if I proved myself, that I would not be as hurt because my dad bailed out on us. But...I feel like I can't move on. Not until I learn why he left."

"Do you understand that even if I find him - that I cannot guarantee results? Your father might not want to talk to you."

"That isn't news to me," she said, and with a bit of sass. "But this here...is a root cause analysis to my stunted existence. Do you know what a root cause analysis means?"

"Believe it or not, I do."

I knew that a root cause analysis meant an in-depth investigation into the causes of problems to come up with answers to solving those problems.

Talks with my friend Angie introduced me to business and psychological terms given to problem and solution exploration. While my friend's current occupation was that of a Wicca store owner, she was a psychologist who kept her license active.

"Oh. Well, okay. Finding out that my dad is an asshole might not resolve my childhood feelings of being abandoned," Amanda added. "But it's a start. I can't carry on with my life until I face him - or face the fact that he doesn't want to talk to me and my sister. I need to resolve this, though. To do that, I need data."

"Your argument is absolutely solid."

Amanda's eyes widened. "So, you'll take my case?"

"Let me ask you a few more questions."

"Shoot."

"How old is your father?"

"He's quite older than my mother. He'd be about seventy-two years old right now."

"Wow," I whispered.

"He was pretty handsome," Amanda said as she showed me a picture on her cell phone. "Agustin Trujillo," she said by way of introduction.

The man was handsome. I stared at his face for a bit. Judging by the smile on his face, Agustin knew he was a good-looking man.

"So, he was in his late forties when he married your mother, right?"

Amanda let out a breath. "They never actually married. But you are right about the age."

"How many older siblings do you have - your father's previous children?"

"Why do you think he had other kids?"

I waved the picture a bit. "I'm not trying to stereotype here, but...it was a hunch. A strong one."

"Four kids before us. All boys."

"Are they a part of your life?"

"No. I couldn't even pick them out of a line-up. I think they live here in Chicago somewhere."

I set the man's picture down and stared at my pad. It was time to ask hard questions.

"Amanda. Has it occurred to you that maybe his disappearance - your father bailing out - was for the best?"

"I have. Still, Agustin Trujillo is my dad. I am owed answers."

"He might bring trouble to your life."

"I'm a big girl, Marta. I can handle Agustin Trujillo."

That remained to be seen.

"I am going to tell you something I tell all of my clients."

"Does that mean you are going to take my case?"

"Hear me out, Amanda. You might not want the answers this investigation will provide. My findings might leave you in a worse place than you are now."

"That's up to me," Amanda said, full of sass. "If I pay you, you'll deliver – or do your best. Am I right?"

"What did your mother say about your father?"

Amanda's bluster died. "Mom died last year. Like I said before, for years she swore he would come back. But he didn't. Then something happened a couple of years before she passed. Mom changed her tune. She said that it was best that me and Becky did not have him present."

Crap. That intrigued me.

"Did your mother say why she changed her mind?"

Amanda shook her head. "No. She didn't."

I stared at Amanda for a bit. “Okay. Three hundred dollars cash in a non-refundable deposit.”

Amanda sighed in relief. “Thank you – for taking my case and giving me a reduced rate.”

“Well, we are talking about a deposit. If this case gets busy or requires a lot of man hours, I will need more money.”

“If you can defend the reasons why you need more money, I can provide it.”

I stared at Amanda a bit longer and then glanced down at her cell phone.

“Okay. Can we talk about what you did and how weird it is?” I whispered.

Amanda blushed and nodded. “You mean the Facebook thing, right?”

The image Amanda provided for me was a Facebook profile picture. Amanda had made a Facebook page for her father.

I nodded. “Yeah. I don’t even know what the legalities are there. You made a page where you are impersonating your father.”

Amanda shook her head. “But I didn’t use his real name. Just ‘A. Trujillo.’ Also, that picture is mine. My mother left it to me and Becky.”

I groaned and sat back. “I don’t know all of the privacy or maybe intellectual property laws that might come with this. I know people who do,” I said as I thought of Kevin and Jane, “but, I am not going to bother them with this.”

Amanda shrugged. "Okay. Fine. In the grand scheme of things, I did something sketchy. But who is worse? Me, for trying to find my father, or my father for abandoning my mother, me, and my sister?"

I shook my head. "That's a topic for theologians or philosophers. Maybe a psychologist. Worst-case scenario, a prosecutor."

"Fine!" Amanda angrily said. "But you have to admit that what I did worked. You're a private investigator. You can't tell me that you've always done above-the-board stuff to find answers."

Amanda wasn't wrong.

"Okay. I'm done giving you a hard time. What I'd like now is for you to tell me – from the top – everything that happened after you made a Facebook profile for your father."

"I can do that," Amanda said as she nodded. "So," she said as she grabbed her mug of coffee. "I made a Facebook profile page for my dad. I tagged some of his old friends in it. I added cities where he's lived – Milwaukee, Waukesha, and Chicago. I added occupations and places where he's worked."

Amanda leaned back and made eye contact with a waitress. A minute later, both of our mugs were refilled.

"I am not on FB much myself," Amanda continued. "That's for older people. No offense!" Amanda said as she widened her eyes and stared at me.

I shook my head. "None taken."

"I prefer Insta myself. But, like I was saying, I checked my dad's page every week or so. One day, I got a notification for his page. FB wanted to tag him in a picture they'd found of him."

"Wow," I said as I stirred some sugar into my coffee.

Amanda laughed. "I know. So, I look up the picture. It was at a Hibachi-style restaurant. You know what those are?"

"I do."

"Yeah, so the picture wasn't taken by my dad or anyone with him. It was a woman who was there in the same grilling area as my dad! She was taking a picture of some guy, but my dad was in the background with some woman. How crazy is that?"

I laughed. "That's pretty crazy. Social media is crazy."

Amanda had the grace to blush. "Yeah. I know what I am doing is messed up."

"Stop apologizing. The profile was a tool you used to solve a problem."

"Cool. So, looking at that hibachi restaurant picture of my dad? I figured out the date, time, and location of the place. It's a good starting point, right?"

I sighed. "It is. I don't know how much information that picture will give me, but I'll work with it. Why don't you go ahead and mail me a picture of your dad, as well as a copy of that Facebook picture of him at the restaurant?"

"Oh, I can just text them to you right now," Amanda said as she reached for her phone.

I shook my head. “No. Do not text those to me.”

Amanda’s shoulders dropped. “Yeah. Um. I guess you don’t want to get in trouble with the cops.”

“I don’t even know if you’ve committed a crime,” I whispered to her. “But I have to take care of myself.”

I reached for one of my sleuthing cards – one that had only my phone number and P.O. Box on it.

“Mail the pictures to this address. Make sure they are high-resolution prints, too.”

Amanda took my card and nodded. “I’m learning a lot – just sitting here with you.”

“You don’t want sleuthing tips, though; you want your father.”

“I do. Can I mail you a personal check?”

“No. Cash only,” I said by way of answer.

Amanda blinked long (probably false) eyelashes at me. “Cash? Are you for real?”

“I am.”

Amanda let out a breath. “Okay. Fine. My bank’s got an ATM right down the road. Can you wait here for about fifteen minutes?”

I nodded. “Sure. But make it ten. I have somewhere I need to be.”

Twenty-five minutes later held me sitting on my couch, remote in hand. I was about to turn the TV on when my phone rang.

"Yeah, Mami. I'm here; I'm about to turn it on."

"What are you about to turn on?" asked my boyfriend.

I groaned. "Darn. I didn't look at my phone before I answered it."

"Oh, good. Because that doesn't sound suspicious at all."

"No. It's not like that. There's a…thing I've been watching. With my mom."

"What have you been watching?"

Kevin's voice was full of indignation.

"Why do you want to know?" I asked.

My phone beeped. I looked and saw that it was my mom calling. I rolled my eyes and ignored the call.

"Stop answering questions with questions."

"Why do you need to know what I am watching?"

"Why are you keeping it from me?"

"It's a *novela*, okay? I've been watching a cheesy *novela* with my mom."

"I don't know if I believe that."

I hit pause on my TV and stood up. "It's the truth."

"What's it called?" he challenged.

I groaned. "It's called *¿Quién ama a Ana Luz?*"

"Who loves the light?" Kevin asked.

I almost laughed, but didn't, as Kevin was being pushy.

"No. 'Who loves Ana Luz?' That's the name of the novela."

"Hold on. I'm googling that."

"No. I'm not going to hold on."

"Marta? Give me a minute."

"No. I'll call you later. Like in an hour. Bye."

So, for better or worse, I hung up on my boyfriend and turned my TV on. My mom called back and had questions.

"I had another call."

"With whom?"

"No talking. It's time for the show."

Kevin, of course, showed up about fifteen minutes after I hung up on him. Sighing, I hit pause on the TV.

"You hung up on me," he said as he hung up his jacket (and weapon) on a hook by the door.

I shrugged and got up to greet him.

"Don't be so enthused to see me," he quipped.

"I'm sorry. I was watching my show."

"What are we watching again?" he asked as he sat down on the couch and grabbed the remote.

I withheld a groan and reached for my phone. "Mom? I am going to have to call you back. Love you."

"*¿Que paso*?"

"*Nada*. I'll call you later."

Moments later, Kevin and I were watching Ana Luz arguing with the interior designer she worked for. Kevin – brow furrowed – sat forward in his seat.

"Do you need me to put English subtitles on?" I asked him.

"Don't insult me," was his answer.

Kevin hit pause and stared at the screen. "So…is the pretty brunette the protagonist?"

"She is," I said as I rubbed the back of my neck.

"I take it that the effete interior designer is her boss."

I nodded. "Yeah."

"Okay. So, she's trying to talk her boss into installing sharp metal lawn sculptures on that beach property?"

"Yeah," I drew out.

"In Puerto Rico. Ana Luz wants to install eight-foot flying knives smack dab in the middle of a beach in Hurricane Alley?"

I smiled. "Yeah. I guess."

"How smart is she supposed to be?"

Of all things, I laughed. "I don't know. It's a question that me and my family explore. Like, every night."

Kevin turned to face me. "You watch this every night?"

I nodded. "Yeah. My mom 'watches' it with me," I air-quoted as I pointed to a cell phone. "My dad, in turn, watches it with her. My brother and sister-in-law watch it when they can. We all get on the speakerphone and talk about it as we watch it."

"Oh," Kevin said as he turned back to the TV. After a moment of silence, he turned the TV back on.

We watched the show in silence, which was not what I was used to. When it was done, Kevin turned the TV off but said nothing.

"Hey. What's on your mind?"

"Is this why you haven't been agreeing to dates at this time of night?"

I sighed. "You caught onto that."

"Of course I did," Kevin said as he turned to me. "Why have you been keeping this from me?"

I shrugged. "It's kind of trash TV. I didn't want to have to explain myself."

"I feel…unincluded."

That made me feel guilty. "I wasn't trying to make you feel that way."

"It's a family thing…but I wasn't invited," he said as he stood up.

Crap. Were we getting into a fight?

"No. It's…a guilty pleasure – the key word being *guilty* – that we all started watching. It wasn't a family thing to begin with. My mom started watching it first. She talked about the marvel of the writing, which I didn't believe because it's a *novela*. But…I watched it with her. It became a thing we shared. Then, I learned that my brother was watching it. Dad was eavesdropping on my mom's speakerphone calls to me, which I was unaware of," I said as I stood up.

"Am I a part of your family?" he asked of me.

Okay. Great. We were fighting.

"I love you," I said to him.

"I know that, but that's not what I asked."

"You are my emergency contact. You have a key to my apartment."

"Am I your family?" he angrily asked.

Fine. Mr. Bossy Detective was about to get his answers.

"You KNOW the answer to that. I want you as a family member so bad that I want to be your wife!" I barked. "But you haven't proposed. I don't even know if you want to marry me. I don't know if you are going to propose. I don't know why you haven't proposed."

Kevin blinked a few times. "So, you're turning this around on me?"

"No. I'm a grown woman and I can account for my actions. I'm sorry I didn't tell you about the novela and how I was watching it with my family. I am sorry I didn't invite you to share in it. I could come up with a bunch of reasons why, but I won't. You are mad and hurt that I didn't tell you. I am sorry."

Kevin blushed and rubbed the back of his neck. "Okay. Thanks."

"What about everything else I said?" I said to him.

Kevin's blue eyes widened. "What do you mean?"

"Now you're the one dodging my questions."

Kevin groaned. "Shit's been crazy, Marta. I haven't had time to…do stuff."

"Stuff?" I questioned.

"You know. Stuff," he muttered.

Tears filled my eyes. I wanted to rant and rave at Kevin. If I'd been the Marta of three years ago, I might have. But life was crazy. I didn't have to add to it.

So, I shook my head instead. "You can take your bag and go, Kevin," I said as I pointed to the blue overnight bag by the door.

"Marta. No," he whispered.

"As a matter of fact, you can't stay overnight anymore. Not until we are engaged or married," I said as my voice cracked.

"Marta. You know we are headed there."

"No!" I barked. "No, I do not. I love you, you love me, and I give you nearly everything I have to give. But you won't do the same," I said as I let out a sob. "You need to go."

"Why are we fighting, Marta? Is it because of that novela? I'm sorry we fought over that," he said as he swallowed at something in his throat.

I shook my head. "No. Don't make it about that. We are fighting because you aren't willing to talk about marrying me."

Kevin's eyes filled with tears. "Please, Marta. Let me stay. We will talk about it."

"I don't think you want to talk about it. And I'm tired tonight. I'm tired of arguing."

And I was tired of waiting, but I wasn't going to say that.

"I love you, Marta."

I nodded. "I love you, too. Good night," I said as I swallowed at tears.

I then opened the front door for him. Kevin stood there for a moment. He then grabbed his things, kissed me, and left.

I closed the door behind him and listened as his feet walked down the metal stairs that led to the parking lot below.

"I'm not crying," I said to myself as I wiped my tears. "No," I said as I sobbed. "I'm going to cry."

I walked to the cabinet over my fridge, where I found a bottle of rum. I then opened my freezer and saw that I was out of cheesecake.

I cried in earnest, then.

Chapter Four

I woke up the next morning to puffy eyelids and no cold cucumbers to make them shrink. I settled for the backs of cold spoons to bring the puffiness down.

Kevin and I had talked over the phone after our argument the night before. However, the elephant in the room made it hard to get any worthy conversation in.

I sent Kevin a 'good morning' text but told him that I had to run out and didn't have time to call. The truth was, I didn't want to keep crying.

In my efforts to not come off as a liar, I put casual clothing on and was about to head out the door when my phone rang.

I groaned as I saw Esteban Morales' number there. I was going to ignore the call. Instead, I set my purse down and took a seat on the steps outside of my apartment.

"Hey, Dad," I said by way of answer.

"Hey, Mija. How are you?"

I let out a loud sigh. "Is Mom eavesdropping right now?"

"No. I am out getting donuts and I thought I'd call you. Are you okay?"

"Not really, Dad."

"Why not?"

"I had a non-fight with Kevin," I said as I absentmindedly messed with the shoelace on my right sneaker.

"What's a non-fight? How's it different from a fight?"

"It's a small fight that hides within it a larger fight."

"Oh. What was the larger fight?"

"Marriage, Dad. I thought we'd be engaged by now. Kevin hasn't wanted to talk about it. I mean, he kind of promised we'd be engaged by now, but we aren't."

"Ah," was Dad's answer.

"Yeah. It's been on my mind for a while now, I guess. I blew up over it last night."

"You know that most American men – Hispanics included – are okay with shacking up. Having children out of wedlock, too."

"That's generational. I'm not of that generation, Dad."

"I know you aren't. Kevin is going to have to figure out if he's willing to do what it takes to keep you."

"Yeah," I whispered.

"Enough about your boyfriend. What else are you into?"

I chuckled. "I got a new case, Dad. This one is very interesting. Still, I think it's going to be a tricky one to solve."

Dad was surprisingly quiet.

"You still there?" I asked.

"Yeah. Look, I can't wait to hear about the case, but there's something I have to get to right now. We'll talk later tonight."

I nodded. "Okay. That works for me. Love you."

"Love you, too, *beba*."

I stared at my phone, long after I'd stopped talking to my dad. I'd been at odds with my father, but that conversation with him left me feeling oddly uplifted. Smiling, I hung up the phone and went back to my apartment to get ready for the day.

Jane was at her condo when I showed up.

"Your face looks puffy and swollen," said the skinny, chic, blonde lawyer.

"Rude," I said as I closed the door to her kitchen.

"What's going on?" she asked as she sat her briefcase down on one of her barstools.

I always started Jane's condo cleaning with the kitchen. There were a few plates in the sink and some stuff on the counter. Still, it would take no time to wash them.

I bent over and retrieved the dishwashing gloves before getting started with her dishes.

"You know a small fight that disguises a bigger one?"

"I know them very well. Do you forget that I'm a lawyer?"

"You won't let me," I said without looking at her.

Jane laughed, which made me smile. "Did the marriage fight finally happen?"

"Kind of. But it was one-sided. I cut through the crap that was the smaller argument and got to the heart of things. Not only is Kevin not ready to propose, he isn't even ready to talk about why. I mean, he says he's ready to talk about it, but I can tell he isn't."

"Huh," Jane muttered.

"What does that mean?" I said as I turned to her.

"I think that maybe he was the one using a small fight to hide something bigger."

Had Kevin been wanting to fight over something else that wasn't marriage or the stupid novela?

"You think he was hiding something?"

"Maybe. Did you ask him if something else was on *his* mind?"

"No," I whined. "He attacked me over secretly blocking an hour out every day and sharing that with my family."

"You didn't include him?"

I blushed. "No. It was to watch a stupid telenovela. My mom got me to watch it and then I got hooked; Mom and I would talk on speakerphone during that hour of watching the soap opera. It was nice. Then my brother and my dad jumped in on the novela and the phone call. It felt like I was in the room with them, and not in another country."

"Okay. So maybe you should have told him about the daily meetings with your family. Maybe he would have felt included."

"But it wasn't a deliberate thing. It just happened."

"Did you deliberately keep it from him?"

"Yeah. I guess," I said as I dropped the dishrag into the sink.

Jane nodded and drummed her fingers on her countertop. "Okay. I think that by now, your heads have cooled. Kevin will have realized that he had a hissy fit over what was the only family time you could share being that your family is overseas. He probably feels bad about it. You have realized that you should have told Kevin about the new ritual. He would have liked to be invited – or at the very least told about it. That's not to say that the marriage fight is not the underlying issue. *That* issue is not going to resolve itself right now, anyway. But you could make peace with each other on the other stuff."

I deflated. "Counselor: how much do I owe you?"

"I left the crap in the fridge for a Mississippi Pot Roast. Make that for me and we'll call it good."

Jane got up from her chair, shot an imaginary gun at me, and then left her condo.

As I drove to my haberdashery/pawn shop clients, I called Kevin.

"Hey you," he said to me.

"Hey yourself. How was your night?"

He let out a breath. "Not great. I fought with my girlfriend, so I slept like crap."

I swallowed at a frog in my throat. "I'm sorry I didn't tell you about the novela. Would you like to come and watch it with…us tonight?"

"It's kind of a crappy novela, Marta."

I groaned. "I know! But you wanted to be invited."

"No. I wanted to be *told* about it. I wanted the option."

"And I am giving it to you now."

Kevin was quiet for a while.

"Barring the whole marriage argument," I said as I blushed. "Is there anything else on your mind?"

Kevin let out a breath. "Nothing that can't wait. I'm not trying to blow you off here, but one of my cases is going to shit. The captain handed me my ass last night."

Instantly, I was sorry that I had not noticed Kevin's distress the night before.

"I am so sorry. What can I do?"

"Nothing to be done right now, save for working. So damned much."

I swallowed at another knot in my throat. "You know where to find me."

"I do. Look; I got to go."

"Okay. I love you."

“I love you.”

So, we hung up. With no plans for the immediate or distant future. I would have to stop and get some cheesecake on the way home.

Chapter Five

After finishing my last cleaning gig for the day, I met up with Ada – my soon-to-be-ex financial planner.

"You are humoring me this evening," Ada said as she got up and hugged me.

I laughed and hugged her back before sitting down at the table at the Panera Bread restaurant she was so fond of.

"I know," I said as I sighed. "Also, I was at a nicer café yesterday, so there's that."

"Ouch!" Ada complained.

I laughed and stirred the coffee I'd ordered.

"So. This is our last meeting," Ada said as she sighed. "I am so sorry for that."

I shrugged. "You work for my ex-husband Anibal, who is paying you to see me for free."

Anibal, my ex-husband, was a certified public accountant. He was the father of our deceased son, Hector. We'd split up a million years ago when I couldn't stop being angry with him and he couldn't stop sleeping with his secretary. I was mature enough to own the fact that I messed up first. Still, Anibal carried a candle for me – even after divorcing me, marrying his secretary, and having two kids with her. It might have been affection that made him worry about my financial prospects, or it might have been out of a sense of duty to our deceased son.

Whatever the cause of Anibal's concern for me, it had to stop. Because it was weird.

“Anibal pulled me into his office yesterday,” Ada said as she pushed her glasses up her nose.

“Uh-oh. That’s how he found his last wife, you know.”

Ada laughed out loud – and hard. “Stop it, you!”

I laughed, too. “What did Anibal want?”

“He wanted me to tell you how much he wanted you to keep me as a financial planner. He said that if it was the money, that you could pay me – at a discounted rate.”

I shook my head. “Anibal is still your boss, though. It’s weird. I have to move on.”

“No,” Ada said as she shook her head. “He does not have access to my records. They are private.”

My smile faded. “Anibal needs to move on.”

Ada let out a breath. “You are probably right. But you have to promise me that you’ll use one of my friends. I know they are reliable.”

I nodded. “I will.”

I had a sip of my coffee while Ada looked at her laptop – probably reviewing the receipts I’d sent her.

“Have you been looking at properties?”

I sighed. “Not as of yet, no. I just moved into my apartment – which I love.”

“You are paying more for it than you did for your place at Doña Justa’s.”

"True, but she was going to crank up my monthly rent anyway."

Ada nodded. "You're not wrong. Also, in all fairness, you were probably due for a rent increase anyway."

"I spend slightly less money on gas because of my location. And then there's the nightlife," I said as I smiled.

Ada laughed. "Yeah. I've seen that your theater and restaurant expenditures have gone up."

"So has my piece of mind."

Ada tapped the table a bit. "Have you been watching Adan much – your grandson?"

I nodded. "Yeah. But I haven't seen him in a bit. Waleska – my daughter-in-law – is in Puerto Rico on an extended vacation, so I won't see her for a couple of weeks."

"Had you been watching your grandson for free?"

I nodded. "Yeah."

"Okay," Ada said. "If, for some reason, you were to shuffle around your hours to watch him during the day, I might broach your daughter-in-law to pay you for daycare."

I nearly shuddered at the thought. "I'm not going to do that. She's a single, widowed mother. Also, I can't afford to not clean or…my other activities."

Ada lifted her eyes from her screen as she looked at me. "How's that going?"

"It's going," I said as I blushed. "I'm working on another case. It's interesting, but I can't reveal details."

"I bet it is interesting."

Ada went serious for a moment. "This is tacky and I hate bringing it up. However, in leaving my services, I want you to be in the best position possible."

"That's quite the lead-up. What's your question?"

"Are you going to marry your detective?"

I sighed. "Can you keep a secret?"

"Of course."

"I'd love to marry him. But I haven't been asked."

Ada nodded. "If you were to get married, that would take a financial load off your shoulders. You wouldn't have to worry about paying for housing or health insurance."

"Ada; you aren't wrong. However, I got into this…nearly middle-aged mess by counting on a man and getting too comfortable. I need to build a life where I can rely on myself. Looking at my boyfriend as a safe-landing zone is not the way to get there."

"Which is why you need to find a house. Right now, you are kind of relying on the charity of client Barney. What happens when he dies, huh? I'll tell you what happens. His descendants will inherit EVERYTHING. That apartment you rent is in a prime location. If it were me, I'd raze that and put up a four-plex condo. That's why you have to buy a house. You will protect yourself then."

I let out a breath and rested my face on my hands. After a few moments, I spoke.

"Ada?"

"Yeah, Marta."

"I'm not ready to fire you as my financial advisor."

Ada laughed, which made me look at her.

"I'm glad. You need me to kick you in the butt," she whispered.

"However, I am going to have to pay you for your services."

Ada nodded. "You know what? That works. Let's go ahead and schedule an appointment for next week," she said as she looked at her watch. "I got to get home for my show."

I lifted my eyes from my hands and stared at my financial advisor.

"*¿Quién ama a Ana Luz*?"

Ada laughed out loud in answer. "Yes! Who is going to love that bird-brained pretty girl?"

I laughed out loud. "We do! We love her."

"Okay," Ada said as she looked at her laptop. "I'm throwing you in here for an appointment next week. Text me if it doesn't work."

"I have got to go," I said as I stood up.

"Me too!"

Laughing, we dashed for the exit of the restaurant.

That evening, I watched my novela, all the while waiting for Kevin's call. It didn't come during the show. It didn't come right after, either. Over cheesecake and rum, I called him.

"Hey. You okay?" he asked of me.

"Yeah, but I could ask that of you. What's going on?" I asked as I paced my kitchen.

"I'm busy at work. Shit's crazy."

I looked at the calendar and saw that it was Friday.

"Okay. Will I see you tomorrow?"

"Probably not."

A frisson of fear took seat in my belly. "How about for mass on Sunday?"

"I don't know. I'm hoping so."

I sighed and forced myself to be strong. "If you need space after what we…talked or didn't talk about last night, I understand. Just please let me know what you are doing, okay?"

"I'm WORKING, Marta! That's what I'm doing!" he barked at me.

Kevin yelled at me. My sweet detective boyfriend scolded at me in a way that he never had before. So stunned was I that I dropped my phone. I watched as the black plastic square fell from my hand and hit the linoleum floor I stood on. After striking the floor, it broke into a few pieces.

Was it prophetic? Was it a metaphor? What had broken? My heart? My relationship with my boyfriend, or my phone?

I picked the phone up and stared at the screen. The buttons did nothing.

“Goodness. You are as dead as Elvis,” I said.

I grabbed my dustpan and broom and began to sweep up the pieces off my kitchen floor. Five minutes later held my front door opening.

“Marta? Are you okay?” Kevin asked.

“You just let yourself into my apartment,” I calmly said to him.

“You hung up on me and didn’t take my calls. I worried.”

“Worried about what?” I asked as I walked his way.

Kevin swallowed. “I don’t know. But I’m sorry. I should not have spoken to you the way I did.”

“You shocked me so much that I dropped my phone. It broke into four pieces,” I said as I pointed at my trash can. “I…darn,” I said as I took a breath. “I need to go and get a new phone.”

“I’ll buy you one. I’m so sorry,” he said as his voice cracked.

“I’m not letting you buy me a phone,” I said to him.

“It’s only fair. I made you break your other one. Come on; I can take half an hour to go and buy you a new phone.”

I shook my head. “No. I’m not letting you buy me a new phone.”

“Why not?”

"Because I am mad at you," I said to him. "You don't get to make things right by buying me things. Good behavior gets you in my good graces," I said as my voice cracked.

Kevin sobbed for a moment, which startled me. "I fucked up at work, Marta. I…made a bad call."

Forgetting my anger, I grabbed Kevin by the hand and walked him to my couch. He sank onto it and then leaned back. Ashamed, he covered his eyes with his hands.

Mesmerized, I watched as his body shook. Still, he made no sound. I leaned into him and put my head on his shoulder. He pulled me tightly against him and continued crying. After a few minutes, he let out a shuddering breath.

"Tell me about it?" I whispered.

"One of my covert informers was killed."

"Oh, wow," I whispered.

"I thought my…investigation was going in one direction. I got distracted by stupid, mundane shit, Marta. I thought my guy was okay. He said he was. He got himself killed. I got him killed."

I looked into Kevin's watery, bloodshot eyes and opened my heart to him.

"I know you can't tell me details, Kevin, but I trust your judgment. Things must have been bad if something got away from you like that."

Kevin shook his head. "Don't give me too much credit, Marta. I'm not as sharp as you."

I sighed. "No one is."

Kevin chuckled and then wiped his eyes. I laughed.

"Look at how frigging blue your eyes look right now. It's ridiculous. I hope you don't take your good looks for granted."

Kevin laughed out loud. "Stop it. You can't make me laugh this hard after I just fell apart on your couch."

"No one is sharp all the time, Kevin. There's always something out there, ready to trip me up. I miss things when I am arrogant. I make mistakes when I let my feelings overcome my judgment." For a moment, I thought about my father. "Look at my dad. He had my entire family fooled."

"You haven't talked about him much of late."

"I'm trying to get past my anger with him. It's working. But that wasn't my point. My dad – brilliant man that he is – thought that he'd fooled me and my brother. And he did. For years. But someone else spilled the beans. My dad was so shocked when I told him I knew. He became a mess and…made another mess because of his arrogance."

Kevin grew comfortable enough to gently tug at the curls that had escaped my bun. It was giving me chills on my neck and in other regions.

"So, what you're saying is that everyone messes up. Maybe so, but I got someone killed," he somberly said.

"Did you, or did he get himself killed?"

"Doesn't matter. It was on my watch," he said as he released my tendril and leaned forward on my couch.

I let out a breath. “I’m sure there are lots of cliches I could throw out right now. I wish I could do your work for you. I wish I could look through your files and point you in some sort of direction, but I can’t do that because I am not a Chicago police detective. I don’t have the education or the experience. You do. You have to…get off this couch and get back at it. Fight through this case until it’s done and then take some time off.”

Kevin let out a breath and then stood up. He grabbed my hand and pulled me up.

“Are you serious about not letting me buy you a phone?”

“Yeah.”

“I’m so sorry I yelled at you. You don’t deserve that.”

I nodded. “Thank you.”

“I am equal parts proud and scared of your independence.”

That surprised me. “Really?”

“Yeah. You have me, but if you didn’t, you’d be fine.”

“Don’t be cavalier about that.”

Kevin shook his head. “Forget I said that. I’m kind of a mess right now.”

“What else was on your mind yesterday?” I asked as I gently grabbed his hand.

"Well, it was a couple of things. The case going to shit and…a vacation."

"What kind of vacation?"

Kevin sighed. "My mom's brother is in a bad way. He's in Cork over in Ireland. My parents want me to go with them to see him. I don't know if I am supposed to have you come along or not and that's kind of my fault."

I let out a breath. "Okay."

Kevin nodded. "I'm not stringing you along, Marta. And it's not like I need time to make up my mind. It's just that that kind of undertaking takes time that I don't have right now."

"Do you mean proposing or the wedding act itself?"

"Both."

I let out another breath. "Okay. Go to Ireland without me. I'll be here. Or maybe in Puerto Rico, but I will still be yours. Unless you make me break another phone."

"I can't tell if you're joking or not."

"I can't either."

Kevin groaned and let out a shuddering breath.

"I'm serious, though; go back to work and make sense of your case. Go to Ireland without worrying about whether or not I should go with you. It's not like I can take the time off my cleaning gigs or my new sleuthing gig, anyway."

"New sleuthing gig?" he asked, and a bit testily.

I nodded. "Yeah. I got a referral."

"From whom?"

Great. Kevin had gotten his pissy detective confidence back.

"A former client. Waleska in Great Lakes?"

"The witchcraft case by the Naval Station up that way. Who is she referring you to? What's this case? Is it local?"

"Local."

"Chicago? Fucking Chicago?" he barked.

"Profanity," I meekly whispered.

"I'm going to have to put a lot of time into the confessional booth anyway, all the cussing I've done. But don't try to sidetrack me. What kind of Chicago jobs are you taking?"

"I'm helping someone find her father."

"Is he a criminal? Is she a criminal?"

I shook my head. "No. She's a professional and stuff. Aside from being a deadbeat, I don't know what her father is into."

Kevin paced for a moment. "If he's a criminal, you are to back out of this case. I don't mean it as a possessive boyfriend, but as someone who deals with psychotic Chicago criminals on the daily."

"How do you have time to stand here and argue with me about this stuff? Isn't your captain breathing down your neck?"

Kevin shrugged. "I left my work phone in the car. But I'm serious, Marta."

I nodded. "You know what? You are right about my needing to research my client further."

"I'm right about a lot of stuff here, Marta."

"I need to go out and buy a new phone," I said, a bit of testiness in my tone.

Kevin deflated. "I am so sorry."

"You go back to work and get your case done. And then you make mass with me on Sunday, Kevin."

Kevin nodded. "I will. I promise."

Kevin leaned down and kissed me twice. "Can I keep my key?"

I shrugged. "For now."

He kept staring at me.

"I am serious about that, Kevin. I can handle your rough edges, but I won't be roughed up."

He kissed me again. "I won't do that again. I love you."

"I love you," I said as I sighed. "Go."

So, he did.

Sadly, I felt better once he was gone. It wasn't his absence that gave me peace, but the knowledge of what he was doing. Kevin needed to get back into the thick of things at work for a bit. I needed my space from him so that I could buy a new darned phone.

He needed to go to Ireland with *his* family. Maybe there, he could muster the energy to make a new family with me.

Kevin wasn't wrong about my looking into Amanda Trujillo, either.

"You're slacking, Marta," I grumbled.

With that in mind, I dashed out – and walked down the street – to the twenty-four-hour pharmacy to buy a new phone. I splurged and paid for a rubber cover for it, too.

Once I got home, I switched my SIM card from my broken phone to my new one.

"All set up," I muttered. "You owe me, Kevin Connelly."

I shelved my still-charging phone and pulled out my laptop. From there, I hit up Facebook using the bare-bones fake profile I had made for myself.

Awilda was a Facebook friend already; I leap-frogged over Awilda's friends until I found Amanda Trujillo's profile.

My new client's profile was pretty active.

"Huh," I muttered. "Only on Insta my butt," I muttered.

I got up and went to a drawer in my kitchen, from which I retrieved a manila folder and a legal pad. I saw pictures on Amanda's profile that showed her traveling. Another young lady who looked a lot like Amanda had her name tagged to the pictures – Rebecca Trujillo. I'd found Amanda's sister.

"But what can I tell about your life, Amanda?"

I looked at her public pictures and saw many images of certificates and awards. A nice late-model Honda was featured, as well as a luxury townhome.

"You're showing off. For whom? For your dad?"

I jotted down some notes about what I detected about her. I then went to her sister's profile and did the same. Her sister – Becky – appeared to be a bit less decadent and showy.

"Becky is…satisfied. She isn't showy. She has no one to impress," I said out loud. "Why is she missing the daddy issues you have, Amanda?"

I didn't get answers, but wrote my thoughts down. Thinking quickly, I called my brother.

"Hey. Where were you for the stupid novela?" Rafy asked.

"I watched it, but couldn't gab. Didn't have the energy for it."

"Telenovela watching is not optional. Slinging mud at the show is the family pastime."

I chuckled. "I know. But I had something to deal with here at home."

"Man trouble?"

I grunted. "Kind of. It is somewhat resolved. Or maybe not. Crap takes time and stuff."

"Word. Why'd you call?"

"Are you on Instagram?"

"Hell, yeah. How do you think I keep up with the trends?"

"Can an Instagram account be linked to a Facebook account?"

"For sure. Lots of folks do that."

I nodded. "Okay. Opinion time. Do you think that impersonating someone else on Facebook is a crime?"

"Fuck. What are you getting into now?"

I blushed. "Just a question. I'm not creating a profile."

"As far as I know, it is not a crime. That depends on the state, though, and the reason why. The social media site might have its own rules, too. Doing that kind of crap is trouble waiting to happen."

Crap. Finding Agustin Trujillo might mean trying to keep Amanda safe.

Deciding to buckle down on my work, I got off the phone with my brother.

I did a Google search for people sharing Amanda's dad's name. I got a lot of hits, but nothing that could connect the name-bearers to Amanda Trujillo.

Thinking quickly, I texted Amanda on my sleuther phone and asked her when I could expect the pictures. She quickly replied – saying that she'd overnighted them and that I should get them Saturday morning.

"That works."

I was about to do my dishes when I heard a knock at my door.

“What the eff?” I asked.

The only person that could be at my door would be Kevin. Waleska and Adan were in Puerto Rico. Anibal – my ex-husband – did not know where I lived. My old landlady didn’t know where I lived. Jane knew where I lived as did Angie, but neither would come over without checking in first. My landlord would never bother me at such an hour.

Kevin would have just let himself in, though.

Carefully, I approached my front door. Nervously, I peered through the peephole. What I saw there shocked the hell out of me. Still, I quickly undid the deadbolts on the door and threw it open.

“Dad? What are you doing here?”

“Hey. Can’t a father come and visit his daughter?”

Chapter Six

Shocked, I stepped aside and let my dad in. Even more surprising was the small carry-on he had with him.

"Dad? What are you doing here?" I again asked.

"Am I unwelcome?"

I shrugged. "No. Of course not."

"How about a hug?"

I smiled and hugged him. Five minutes later held us drinking coffee and eating cheesecake.

"I've been making better inroads with your brother, being that he lives down the road from me. With you – due to distance and your personality – I have had to work harder. That's why I am here."

"But what about Mom?" I asked him.

Dad shrugged. "She's fine. I'll be back there soon enough. As a matter of fact, I should probably call her. She doesn't know I came out here."

"Daddy!" I barked.

He ignored me and stood up from the table.

"Can I make this call in your room?"

I sighed. "Yeah. Of course. Go ahead."

In shock, I sent Kevin a quick text. He called me back a minute later.

"Your father's here? In Chicago?" His voice was filled with incredulity.

"Yeah."

"At your apartment?"

"Yes," I said.

"You didn't tell me he was coming."

"*I* didn't know he was coming. He just showed up!"

"Wow. I'm surprised your mom was able to keep that a secret."

"My mom didn't know. I think my dad just packed a bag and came."

"Oh, wow. Wow. Um. Okay. I've got to go, but I'll call you tomorrow morning."

"Okay. Love you."

"Me too."

"And you CANNOT miss mass," I stated.

"I won't."

With that, I hung up with him. After that, I called my brother.

"Dude. Can you look at a fucking clock? Also, wc talked today already," Big Brother rudely said to me.

"Ask me where our father is."

I heard the sound of a lamp turning on. I also heard protests coming from his wife Wanda.

"What are you talking about?"

"Ask me where our father is," I repeated.

"I don't need to! He's right down the road. Right?"

I stepped closer to the door that led to my bedroom. I held the phone out so that Rafy could hear my dad yelling at my mother from the comfort of my bedroom. After a few seconds, I put the phone back on my ear.

"Marta? What is going on?"

"Dad decided to pay me a visit."

"What? What the fuck? He didn't tell me. Mom didn't tell me."

"Oh, he didn't tell anyone. I think he packed a bag, got a ride to the San Juan Luis Muñoz Marin airport, and flew to Chicago O'Hare International Airport."

I could hear Rafy pacing. "Oh my God. Dad's losing his mind. He's going senile. Is it Alzheimer's? It runs in the family! But he's healthy!" Rafy protested. "Shit. Do I need to go out there and get him? What time is it? It's eleven o'clock. I can catch a flight and be there in the morning. Can you watch him until then?"

I heard Rafy's wife Wanda placating him in the background.

"Rafy? Relax," I calmly said. "Dad seems perfectly lucid."

"This is rash and crazy, Marta! What the hell is he doing?"

Surprising me, Dad left my bedroom and reached for my phone. “Could I?” He inquired.

I nodded and handed him the phone. “Rafael. Calm down,” Dad loudly said into my phone. “I didn’t tell anyone I was leaving because I am an adult man. No; I told your mother I was coming to see your sister. I simply didn’t say when. Goodbye.”

Moments later, Dad handed me my phone. “Marta? You call me – tomorrow morning,” Rafy said. “I want to know how Dad spent the night. But I have to go to Mom’s house now. She’s blowing up Wanda’s phone.”

“Why not just pick her up and have her stay at your place?”

“Not a bad idea. I’ll go and get her.”

“Okay. Keep me posted.”

So, I hung up the phone and stared at my dad.

“What did mom say?”

“Nothing I’d care to repeat in polite company.”

Seconds later, my phone rang. It was my mom. I groaned and picked it up.

“Hi, Mami.”

“I don’t understand why he would do this to me. Why couldn’t he tell me he was leaving? Why couldn’t he bring me with him? What is going on in his mind?”

“Mom? Dad’s been here for like fifteen minutes. I don’t have answers for you.”

"You get them and you call me back because your brother's here now."

"Okay, Mom. Good night," I said before hanging up the phone.

I stared at my phone for a while, wondering if another crazy call would come through.

"I knew things would be crazy because of my drop-in visit, but not like this."

I shrugged. "Dad; you know Mom. And Rafy. Mom gets manic and Rafy gets paranoid."

"How do you get?" Dad asked.

I shrugged. "Angry. But then I calm down."

We stared at each other a bit, probably trying to figure out what to do next. Remembering the late hour and my dad's age, I looked at the couch.

"Why don't you go ahead and take the bed, Dad? I'll take the couch."

My father shook his head. "No. I've been banished to the couch many times. I'll be fine on yours."

I shook my head. "No. I insist. My bed is comfortable as is my couch. I'll throw some fresh linens on for you. It'll take me a minute."

Ignoring his protests, I went ahead and removed my bed sheets, placed them on the couch, and then placed fresh ones on my bed. While in my bedroom, I grabbed my shower gear and headed for the bathroom.

"I can't believe how much I am putting you out. I think I saw a motel down the road. I will check in there," my dad said as he stood up from the couch.

I shook my head. "No, Dad. I sleep like the dead. Also, sleeping is the only part that matters. We can get up and have breakfast together and stuff. It'll be fine."

"If you insist."

"I do," was my reply.

Thirty minutes later held me laid out on my couch, not sleeping like a rock, but staring at the ceiling.

It wasn't a terribly uncomfortable couch to sleep in – only mildly so.

"I need to get a pull-out," I whispered to myself.

I wondered what was going on in my father's head. Sure, there was some distance between us owed to his lie about his work history, but we would have overcome that – eventually. What would make him so desperate to get things better between us that he would jump on a plane and not tell anyone?

I thought about calling my brother, but disregarded the notion, as it was past midnight in Puerto Rico.

My phone – which was on silent – vibrated in my hand. I smiled as I saw my brother's number on there.

"Hey," I whispered.

"Hey yourself," my brother said. "What's the story?"

"I let Dad have my bedroom. I'm sleeping on my couch."

Rafy grunted. "Been there. How does he seem?"

"Well, he was excited when he got here. I think. But now he seems a bit sheepish owed to how everyone's reacting."

"Mom was so pissed," Rafy grumbled. "She wouldn't come home with me but insisted on staying at her house. I think she's madder that Dad left her behind than she is that he left, but she's pretty pissed over that, too."

"What a mess," I grumbled.

"Yeah. And you're at the head of it. Are you being nice to Dad?"

I scoffed. "Of course, I am. I gave him my bed!"

"Alright. I got to get to bed. What a crazy fucking night."

"I know it. I'll keep you posted."

After disconnecting with my brother, I forced myself to close my eyes and go to sleep.

I woke up to the sound of a police car's sirens. Opening my eyes, I saw that the dawn had come.

I groaned as I sat up. "This couch sucks," I grumbled.

Still, I got up and made my way to the bathroom. Once I was done there, I found my father fully dressed and seated at my table.

"What do you say we go and get breakfast? My treat."

I thought about that for a moment. "Works for me."

So, we walked to a diner down my block. My dad looked left and right at all of the establishments around us.

"Wow. I understand the appeal of your apartment. You are in the middle of everything."

I smiled. "It's great. Ada – my financial planner – isn't thrilled over how much I'm spending on nightlife stuff but…you only live once, you know? Even being semi-single as I am," I said as I blushed, "I am having fun. I can get a bite to eat for dinner. I can have a drink at a bar and start a conversation with someone. Or I can catch a movie or just browse the shops."

A handful of minutes later held us seated at a small diner table.

"How are things going with your detective boyfriend?"

I sighed. "Well, he's busy with a big case at work. Of course, he always is," I qualified, "but…he's in a hard spot at work right now."

"Did you guys clear up the air?"

"In a manner of speaking," I said as I stirred some sugar into my coffee. "We are in a weird holding pattern. He's got to finish stuff up at work and then he has to go to Ireland to visit a dying uncle. I guess that after that…we'll talk about what will happen. Or what won't happen," I said as I shrugged.

My dad drank from his coffee cup. “Sometimes all you can do is wait.”

“I know it.”

Over breakfast, I told him about my latest gig. My dad’s brow furrowed as I told him about my client starting a Facebook page for her absent father.

“That’s against a few laws.”

I chuckled. “I imagine so.”

“Your client’s tenacity and cunning are to be admired, though.”

“I know. Right now, I am trying to hone in on who she is before I try to find out where her father is. I have to get a handle on Amanda and her motivations before I hand her someone whom she has so many issues with.”

“You’ve got your work cut out for you, Marta,” Dad said. “You’ve got little to no leads.”

“I told Amanda that I could not guarantee results, but that I would do my best work for her.”

After breakfast, we walked around the block a bit. I took my dad with me to the post office.

“I’ve been expecting this,” I said to my father as I pulled a large envelope out of my post office box.

“Let’s take it back to your place, then,” he said.

From my kitchen table, we reviewed the high-definition pictures Amanda had sent me.

"You know what? Show me Amanda's Facebook page. Show me what you've found on her," Dad requested.

So, I pulled out my laptop and showed my dad the notes I'd taken regarding my observations.

"Do you have a recording of the interview?"

"I do."

"Play that."

So, over coffee and crackers, we listened to the recording of the interview. When it was done, my dad hit stop.

"What's the first question that comes to your mind about this?" Dad asked of me.

I stopped my dad with a hand and then popped a blank tape into my recorder and started recording.

"Amanda's mother and Amanda's sister Becky. Amanda's mom always thought that Agustin would come back. But then she changes her mind one day and says it's for the best. Why? Also, Becky – Amanda's sister. Judging by Becky's Facebook profile, she isn't trying to impress anyone like Amanda is. Does Becky know something that Amanda does not?"

"Maybe so, but maybe not. Amanda is the older child, right?"

"Yeah."

Dad nodded before responding. "Then Amanda has more romanticized memories of her father. Amanda might be trying to reclaim something that is long gone – a childhood with her father. She might find the man who begat her, but she is not going to find what she's lost."

I nodded. “Becky is a pre-med student. She might have taken some psychology courses. She might have learned something that enabled her to let her father go.”

“Or she might know something,” my father said.

I nodded and wrote something down. “I need to talk to Becky.”

“Yeah. You need to get more background on the family – and on your client’s mother – before you try to track this guy down,” Dad said as he pointed to the man believed to be Agustin Trujillo.

I studied the picture for a bit. “What does a father owe their child?”

My father patted my hand, making me look at him.

“If you are talking biology? Once a child is conceived, the father’s work is done. If you are talking about religion, morals, and humanity, well, there’s more to it than that.”

My dad pulled his hand back and stared at me a bit. “I jumped on a plane to come out here because our distance pains me. I don’t just mean geographically, but our relationship.”

I sighed. “I know. I’m sorry.”

“Does a parent owe their child the truth? All the time?”

I wasn’t pissy over the question. I shrugged. “I don’t know. Do they?”

My father shook his head. “No. Let me talk about myself in order to make you understand. If we are talking about my identity, I am a seventy-year-old, married, Catholic, Puerto Rican male. I am intelligent to a fault. My personality has been a determining factor in my life choices."

"I've made decisions others might find fault in, but I did what I had to to support my family. Yes, I was a federal agent. I never told you and your brother. I don't think it was a lie of omission. A lie of omission means the intentional exclusion of important information. While my being an FBI agent was important information – it was only important to me. In no way at all did it affect yours or your brother's upbringing."

"You are right in that you did not owe my brother or myself the truth regarding your past as a federal agent. I didn't have a right to be pissy, and I'm sorry."

"Thank you."

"I wasn't done talking. Can you honestly tell me that the FBI has not kept tabs on you, Mom, Rafy, or myself? Throughout our lives?"

My father let out a breath. He then sat back. "I can't. Yes; the FBI has kept tabs on myself, and at times, you and your brother. My past work for them has not been the cause of their focus on you, Marta. You did that on your own."

I blushed as I thought about the two times I'd tangled with the FBI – when I reported the Visions of Teeth identity theft ring, as well as the porch pirate ring.

"You are the most cunning of my children. However, the FBI features agents that are just as canny, if not more so. You need to decide if your adventures are worth being in the FBI's sights."

I thought about my father's words for a few long seconds.

"I've chosen a side job that worries my family and my boyfriend. It's probably making the feds watch Kevin, too. And that's not fair."

Dad nodded. "This conversation wasn't supposed to be about our relationship, but I am glad we talked about it. Let's get back to your case. Agustin Trujillo appears to be a man who sprayed his seed like bullets leaving a semi-automatic weapon. Pardon the vulgarity."

I blushed but nodded. "Of course."

"You cannot expect accountability or feelings of fatherhood from a creature such as this one," Dad said as he pointed to Agustin's picture. "Amanda Trujillo's three hundred dollars will pay for answers, but probably ones that she could have done without."

I was glad I'd recorded mine and my father's conversation. It gave me a direction – talking to Becky's sister. It also restored the order of our relationship. I was grateful for that as I still had more to learn from him.

Chapter Seven

My father and I spent our Saturday driving around and seeing the sights. We drove past Jamie's Pawn Shop and Barney's Haberdashery. We quickly cruised in Jane's neighborhood. Downtown, I showed Dad where Francis Street Cleaners used to be, as well as the big building that housed Smithers and Associates, and even the financial firm where I'd made my first good friend – Melissa Bollinger.

"How's she doing, *beba*?" Dad asked of me.

"I wish I knew. I get a postcard from her from time to time. I think she's working at a financial firm out of Harrisburg, which is the capital of Pennsylvania. She's spending a lot of time with her family."

"Niels Ericsson. Her old boss. Is he giving you trouble?"

I swallowed as I thought about the scary man whom I had made an enemy.

"I've not heard a word from him. He went home to Denmark with his family, though. Also, he made a scene at the police precinct at Blue Island Avenue and in front of no less than three police detectives. I think he'll keep his distance."

"Thank God for small favors."

Suddenly inspired, I drove my dad to Angie's store.

"What in God's name are we doing here?" Dad said as he looked at the Wiccan iconography adorning the glass windows of the store.

"I know," I apologetically said. "I met Angie when I needed help with Awilda's witchcraft case. Angie's become kind of like my best friend. I want you to meet her."

"You are friends with a Wiccan?"

"I'm friends with a non-practicing Catholic who owns a store. She's a psychologist, too. I think that this store is temporary, Dad."

"You need to watch the company you keep, Marta."

I sighed as I parked my car. "Do you not want to meet her?"

"If she's your friend, I will meet her."

So, we walked into the store. Angie beamed at me – leaving a customer by the register to come and greet me with a hug.

"Hey! What a happy surprise!" Angie said as she hugged me. "Who is this?"

I smiled, "Angie: this is my dad – Esteban Morales. Dad this is- "

"Indigo Cassiopeia," Angie loudly said. She then half-smiled and whispered: "You can call me Angie just as soon as this customer leaves."

Dad laughed. "It is nice to meet you, Indigo."

"Let me see to my customer. We'll have tea afterward."

I watched my dad as he stared at a lot of the store's offerings. At a book rack, he poked several books. He picked up a small paperback and read the back cover.

"The writer of this book was arrested and convicted for money laundering," my father said.

Angie, who'd just walked the customer out, came to us. "She wasn't guilty of that. It was her boyfriend who pressured her to commit the crime."

"Guilty is guilty," Dad said as he put the book back into the rack.

"How about culpability?" Angie challenged.

"That only applies to children and the mentally deficient. This author has a B.A. in anthropology and a Master's Degree in sociology."

Angie blinked a few times. "Does she?"

"Yeah," Dad curtly said. "Her social media team scrubbed that from the internet."

"Then how do you know that?"

"I know someone who was present when she was questioned."

Angie pulled the book and stared at the cover. I leaned over and looked at it. It was something about numerology. I chuckled.

"Marta!" Angie complained. "This is serious."

"It's a book on numerology and she was convicted for something having to do with numbers and money. There's a joke in there and you know it."

My dad smiled but looked away. Angie remained serious, though.

"Numerology and money laundering are two separate things. This book in itself is nothing criminal."

"So, don't take it off your shelves," I said to her.

I knew that Angie's business was known to have bad months, so every penny mattered.

"That's not all of it, though. I put this author's book on my shelf because I felt bad that she was being roasted by non-Wiccans. But it seems like the attacks were kind of warranted. The writer painted a picture of what she wanted us to see."

Angie grabbed the author's books with two hands and then took them to the countertop.

"*Ahora me siento mal*," Dad whispered to me.

"We'll make it up to her," I said to Dad. "Hey," I called out to Angie. "You've got an hour until closing. What do you say we go across the street for cinnamon rolls and coffee?"

"I don't know," Angie muttered. "I have inventory that I haven't gotten to, owed to my foster parent classes."

"Well, then, Dad and I will go across the street to get some sweets and coffee and we'll snack and help you do inventory."

Angie smiled. "You have a deal."

Interestingly enough, Angie and my father were the ones who spoke the most. They had a lively debate on religion, crime, criminals, and the penal code. I did most of the counting work, though.

An hour and a half after arriving, I turned to the two of them.

"Well, as *fun* as this has been, we have to go," I said to Angie.

Angie scoffed at me. "It was engaging and worthwhile. Fun is an adjective that is sought out far too much."

"Well said, Angie," Dad said to her.

"Thank you, Esteban. It was a pleasure to meet you. I am going to check those books you told me about."

"It was nice meeting you, too."

With that, we left Angie's store.

"I like your friend, Marta. She's smart and kind."

I smiled. "I do, too."

"But you will need to go to confession tomorrow morning – if you weren't planning on doing so already."

I took a low, slow breath.

"Okay. Why?"

"In patronizing – and helping inventory – a business that goes against Christian values, you are helping sin proliferate."

I groaned. "Fine."

I was quiet for a few moments before something occurred to me.

"We should show up to mass twenty minutes early, though, so that we can both make confession."

"Oh? What do I have to confess?" My dad said, sounding a bit pissy.

"Well, you helped with the inventory. Also, you did kind of leave Mom in a lurch."

My father said nothing, but I could sense his seething anger emanating from his position in the passenger side of my car.

Early the next morning, Kevin texted me, telling me that he would meet me at church.

After dressing, Dad and I left my house and headed for the cathedral downtown.

"What a beautiful church," Dad said as we parked my car.

I smiled. "I think so."

"Where's the boyfriend?" Dad asked as he looked around.

"He'll be here," I said as I blushed.

I left my purse and my sweater in a pew and then joined my father in line for confession. A couple of minutes later, I spotted not one, but two redheads enter the church, along with a blond.

It was Kevin, and his parents were with him. I stared at him – in shock. I watched his eyes widen and then his shoulders gave a low-key shrug.

Kevin mouthed the word "Confession?"

I shrugged and he nodded.

I watched as Kevin touched his mother's arm and pointed in my direction. I blushed and gave a small wave. Kevin's mom nodded and then pointed me out to her husband.

They nodded at me and then followed Kevin to a pew. Kevin sat for approximately three minutes before getting up from his pew and joining the confessional line. His parents watched him with surprise on their faces.

Ten minutes into mass held Dr. Connelly leaving his pew and getting into the confession line as well. Two minutes after that, Mrs. Connelly shrugged and joined the line with her husband.

My confession was laden with feelings of pressure and guilt. After receiving absolution, I sat down at the pew. My father followed shortly after; a while later, Kevin and his parents joined us.

Kevin and I held hands during part of the mass. The unity I felt with him there was a comfort in a somewhat tense time.

After mass, we all stood in the parking lot.

"Dad? This is Kevin. Kevin, this is my dad – Esteban Morales."

Kevin blushed, swallowed, and then firmly shook my dad's hand. "Hello, Mr. Morales. I'm sorry it's taken so long for us to meet."

"The pleasure is mine, Kevin," my father warmly said.

I then introduced Kevin's parents to my dad.

"Dad, this is Dr. Kevin Connelly - Kevin's dad. He's a psychiatrist. This is Kevin's mother, Alice Connelly. She's an attorney."

Everyone shook hands while exchanging pleasantries.

“Marta? Didn’t you say there was a nice diner down the way?” My dad asked of me.

“I did.”

I then looked at Kevin with hopeful eyes.

“Mom? Dad? Join us for breakfast,” Kevin said to his parents as he took a position next to me.

“We would be happy to,” said Mrs. Connelly.

Kevin pulled me aside for a moment, giving me a quick peck.

“I’m happy to see you,” I whispered as I squeezed his hand.

“And I you. Breakfast?”

I nodded. “Yeah.”

Ten minutes later held us in the diner.

“Mr. Morales,” Kevin’s father Kevin Senior said. “What do you do in Puerto Rico?”

“Call me Esteban,” my dad said as he unrolled his napkin from the utensil roll. “I’m mostly retired now. Before retiring, I was involved in insurance adjudication. Prior to that, I did some work for the government that’s best not discussing. These days, I help truck around my twin grandsons to their baseball practices and games.”

"That sounds lovely," Mrs. Connelly said. "I've wondered how different Ireland and Puerto Rico are. They are both island nations."

"Our parents were born in Ireland," Dr. Connelly said.

"So, you are first-generation Americans just like my children," my dad said as he smiled.

Dr. Connelly laughed, as did Mrs. Connelly. "We are."

"Well, Puerto Rico features very intelligent people, but a lot of drunkards who favor fights and violence," Dad said.

"Not at all like Ireland," Kevin dryly said.

Friendly banter occurred while we ate our breakfast. Dad was polite to Kevin and his parents, and they were polite to him.

I, however, felt tense. My sleep the night before had not been great as my couch was lumpier than I remembered. I had no idea when my father was leaving. I wasn't too sure what kind of space I was in as far as Kevin was concerned.

The truth was that I needed some quiet time, but had no idea when I would get it. The answer came in a way that I did not expect.

"So, Kevin; what is tomorrow looking like for you?" my dad asked.

Kevin set his cup of coffee down and stared at my father.

"You mean work?"

"I do," Dad said as he set his napkin down.

Kevin blinked a few times. "Well, I have my case to work on this evening and into tomorrow morning, I imagine. But…if you had something in mind, I could probably carve some time out."

"Do that. I have some old work buddies that would like to meet you."

That only meant one thing. I dropped my fork with a clatter and looked at my father.

"Which work buddies?"

Dad shrugged. "Old work friends. I told them about Kevin and they were impressed."

I glanced at Kevin, whose brow had furrowed. His parents, who had probably learned that my dad used to be a federal agent, looked similarly concerned.

Kevin opened and closed his mouth a few times. I was about to tell my dad that Kevin was too busy when Kevin spoke.

"How does ten a.m. sound?" Kevin politely said.

"That sounds great."

Anger filled me. I stared my father down.

"*¿Que carajo estas tramando*?" I asked of him.

"That's quite the language you are using, and right after mass," my father calmly said.

"Answer my question," I demanded in Spanish.

"Do I need to?"

Quickly, and still in Spanish, I launched accusations and threats towards my father.

My dad let out a low, slow breath, but didn't answer me – in any language.

"Marta," Kevin said as he put his hand on my shoulder. "It's okay. Really."

I turned to him and let out a low slow breath. "It *will* be okay," I said in English.

Dr. Connelly laughed out loud. Kevin groaned, and his mother looked confused.

"The only person at this table who doesn't understand Spanish is my mother," Kevin said to me.

I turned to Mrs. Connelly and nodded. "My apologies, Alice. I questioned my dad's plans and timing."

"I understand, Marta." Mrs. Connelly said as she let out a breath. "That came through."

My dad groaned. "The women in my life try to keep me in line. It doesn't always work, but they try."

I was so angry I could scream. Instead, I shoved my seat back and sct my napkin on the table.

"If you'll excuse me."

I then got up and headed to the ladies' room. I then bypassed that and headed outside. I got on the phone and called my brother.

"Yo," he said.

"If Dad isn't gone from my house by Tuesday, I am sending for Mom."

Rafy laughed and then he groaned. "What's Esteban Morales stirring up?"

I let out a breath. "Can't get into that right now as I am having breakfast with him, Kevin, AND Kevin's parents."

"Oh shit."

"Yeah. Do me a favor and call Mom. Tell her that Dad is plotting."

"Will do."

Two minutes later held me back at the table. Dad was telling a story to Kevin's parents that had them laughing. Discreetly, Kevin put his hand on my knee.

"You okay?" he whispered.

I nodded. "Yeah. You?"

"I'm alright," he answered.

Moments later, my dad's phone rang. His smile fell as he looked at his phone's display. Still, he took the call. Immediately, I heard my mother's strident voice launch into him.

"Your mom?" Kevin asked.

I nodded. "Yeah. She misses my dad. They are very close," I said as I smiled at Dr. and Mrs. Connelly.

My mother's yelling belied my words, though. My father groaned and excused himself before heading outside to finish his call with my mother.

"So, that's Esteban Morales," I said.

Kevin smiled and then laughed. Dr. Connelly and Mrs. Connelly both gave me polite smiles.

After my father settled the tab and gave a warm goodbye to Kevin's parents, he got into my car. I said goodbye to Mr. and Mrs. Connelly who then climbed into their vehicle and departed. A few feet away from my car, Kevin hugged me. I sighed and hugged him back.

"How are things?" he asked as he pulled back and looked me in the face.

"Chaotic. I'm sure they will settle down soon, though."

"Your dad's a card."

"Do not feel obligated to pick him up tomorrow."

Kevin laughed and released me. "It's okay. Really. I want to see what he's trying to pull."

"Be careful. My dad is a plotter."

"I will," Kevin said as he bent down to kiss me. "Will you be working when I pick him up tomorrow?"

"Yes."

Kevin nodded and reached for my hand, wiggling it a bit. It showed his anxiety. It made me feel like he was using me as a comforting mechanism, which I did not mind at all.

"I'm ready for my father to leave," I whispered.

Kevin laughed out loud. "I bet. We have things we need to catch up on."

I raised my eyebrows.

"Not sex," Kevin said as he blushed. "Although, if you're offering, I will take it."

I groaned.

"I mean serious stuff," he said.

I couldn't help but feel like I couldn't trust Kevin. Instead of saying that, I squeezed his hand and released it.

"I have to go. Call me later?"

"Of course."

He kissed me twice and then watched me make my way to my car before heading to his own.

"You two are cute together," Dad said.

I shook my head. "Don't. Not right now."

"Okay."

Once we were back at my apartment, I sank on my couch. I let out a breath that wasn't one of relief, as I was not feeling restful. Sunday was the day of rest, but I couldn't as I had a lot of emotions and events to mentally unpack.

Mass with my dad and Kevin became mass – and breakfast – with my dad, my boyfriend, and my boyfriend's parents. I felt tense throughout breakfast – especially so when my dad decided that it was okay to commandeer Kevin's following workday.

"I think I'm going out for a walk," my father said as he left my bedroom – his bedroom.

"Oh. Um, if you give me a while, I'll go with you."

My father shook his head. “No. I don’t want company – no offense.”

“Okay. How long will you be out?”

“Maybe only a couple of hours. Can I have your car keys?”

“Which one are you doing? Going for a walk or going on a drive?”

“A bit of both.”

I stared my dad down. I felt my blood pressure go up. Then I reminded myself that he had come all the way out to see me. “Alright. Well. Maybe you can call and let me know what your dinner plans are.”

My dad came to me, hand extended. I didn’t want to give him my keys, which made me feel like a hypocrite. Still, I reached into my purse and handed him what he wanted.

“I don’t know if I’ll be back before your dinner. I might get something out.”

Sweet Lord, almighty; Dad was paying me back for my teenage years.

“Bring my car back with a full tank.”

“Will do. Love you, Mija.”

And with that, my dad left.

I stared at the closed door for about five minutes. After that, I got up and called my brother.

“So…he just left?” Rafy said.

“Yes!” I loudly complained.

"He didn't tell you where he was going," Rafy added.

"No. I gave him my car keys and he left," I said as I waved my high-heeled shoe to the door.

"Why did you give him your car keys?"

"Because he asked for them!"

"See, I don't know if I would have done that."

I groaned and threw my other shoe into my closet. "What was I supposed to do? Say no to my father? After Mass? After he came to Chicago to see me? After teenaged me took his car out – so many times?"

Rafy groaned. "Yeah, I can see that, too. But I am not so sure that he only came there to see you. If he had, he'd be with you right now."

In answer, I grabbed my pillow and screamed into it.

So, I changed out of my mass clothing and put something casual on. Then I paced. I thought about calling Kevin to complain but then remembered that he was probably at work.

"That man works too much," I said as I stared at the side of my bed that I hoped he'd sleep on.

I cleaned my kitchen and washed my linens – the ones on my bed and the ones I'd used on the couch.

It was two hours. My father still wasn't back.

I told myself to chill out as I paced my apartment. My dad hadn't been in Chicago since…well, since right around the time my son Hector had passed away.

Did Dad deserve some time exploring? Maybe. But he was retired. What the heck did he do with his time anyway? And where did he need to go with a car? And how was he spending time with me if he was out on his own?

"I can't be here," I muttered to myself.

So, I grabbed my laptop and my cell phone and left my apartment – and hopefully my frustrations – behind.

At a café down the road, I grabbed my sleuther phone and texted Amanda Trujillo, requesting the phone number of Rebecca – her pre-med younger sister. Immediately, my phone rang.

"Hey Marta, this is Amanda."

"Hey Amanda," I said.

"Um. Why do you need to speak to my sister?"

Great. I was getting pushback from Amanda.

"Because I need to know everything she knows."

"My sister doesn't know where my dad is. I already asked her. I told you that."

I let out a low, slow breath.

"I was going to ask her other things."

"Just ask me."

Amanda was starting to piss me off.

"Amanda? Do you want me to find your father?"

"That's what I paid you for."

"If you want me to find your father – quickly – you won't hamper my investigation."

"I'm not doing that. I just don't understand why you want to talk to my sister."

I looked around me and was happy to see that the café was still pretty empty. However, the barista behind the counter seemed to be wiping a spot on a counter nearby with an ardor that was probably unwarranted. She was eavesdropping. Not that I could blame her.

"Look; I can't talk right now," I whispered into the phone. "But be prepared to get part of your deposit back."

"Why?" she asked.

"I can't get into that right now, Amanda. I'll text you later with the next steps. Goodbye."

With that, I hung up the phone. Amanda tried calling me back, then texted me, but I put my phone on silent and ignored it – and Amanda.

Frustration filling me, I packed up my things and went home. When six hours passed without a word from my father, I called Kevin.

"Are you worried about him?" Kevin asked.

I groaned. "No. He's one of the more capable people I know."

"You wondering what he's getting into, huh?"

"I am," I said, frustration filling my voice. "How's he visiting with me when he isn't here? What is he really doing?"

"Well, what's worst-case scenario stuff?"

"Him doing stuff with his fed cronies. Investigating his own crap – while driving my car."

Kevin let out a breath. "Do you want me to put some feelers out there?"

I sighed. "No. I love you for offering that. I just don't think it's time for you to pull out your big guns."

"You know how much I'd love to pull out my big gun on you," he whispered into the phone.

I laughed out loud. "You are a naughty boy."

"You don't know the half of it."

"How were your parents after breakfast?"

Kevin sighed. "Good. My folks were charmed by your father and amused by your antics."

I groaned. "Great."

"Seriously, they were fine. They hadn't been to mass in a minute but were happy they went. I kept teasing them on everything they probably have to do as atonement following confession."

I laughed out loud and Kevin chuckled.

"You don't sound like you are at home."

"Because I am on my way back to the precinct. After breakfast, I went home to shower and get a couple of hours of shut-eye."

"You are working too hard," I kindly said to him.

"I know that," he exclaimed. "What can I do? The one day I hoped to have off to rest and spend time with you was overtaken by all sorts of parents. We have shit to talk about. I don't know what kind of case you are getting into, and I want to know."

Crap. Kevin was still on edge.

"Well, my client is giving me pushback with regards to my interviewing some people close to her, so I am probably going to fire her."

"That's shady on her part, Marta. You should let this case go."

I wanted to tell Kevin that that was my business and that he was being bossy again, but did not want to be argumentative with him while he was feeling tense, and when I didn't know when I'd see him again.

"I don't want to argue."

"Do you think I do?"

"With a question like that and in that tone of voice, I kind of think you do," I snapped back.

"Fuck," Kevin grumbled. "I'm sorry. I need to tone it down. Everything important in my life is on hold while I deal with shit at work. It's fucking pissing me off."

Jane's words from a few days passed came back to mind. Kevin was on a different timeline than I was.

"I'd offer you cheesecake and rum tonight, but…with my dad here, I don't know how relaxing that would be."

"Agreed. Especially since I agreed to his taking me somewhere tomorrow morning."

"I can cancel that for you."

Kevin groaned. "Don't do that. I don't want to alienate your dad. Also, I wasn't lying when I said I was curious about what his peeps had to say."

I sighed. "Parents are dramatic."

"Ha. Who are you telling? Oh, but my folks kind of wanted me to thank you for not coming along to the Ireland trip."

My brow furrowed. "Okay. That's going to take some time to percolate."

Kevin laughed out loud. "That's what I told them. But they wanted me to let you know that this trip is going to be short and sad and not the kind of trip where you get to know people."

"I can understand that."

"And that is why I love you."

I sighed in pleasure over his words. They made the tension and frustration dissipate.

"Would you really go to Puerto Rico without me?"

I shrugged. "If I had to."

"Ouch."

"Are you kidding me right now? You are going to frigging Ireland without me! I'm not having a fit over that!"

"I know. It's just that you've been there twice since we've been dating."

"Uh – false, detective. We weren't dating when I went there a year ago."

"We'd been on *one* date, though, so we weren't *not* dating."

"Kevin," I cut in. "If you put a ring on my finger, you'd have more of a say. It wouldn't be the final word, but your words would have more weight to them."

Kevin groaned and said nothing for a bit.

"Shelving that – for now," I quickly qualified, "I hope you get some rest soon. I know things are crazy at work – and kind of here at home right now," I added as I blushed. "But I don't take your health and safety for granted. I hope you don't, either."

"I don't. It's just that if I put in the time now, shit will get resolved more quickly."

"Okay."

"I just pulled into the precinct. It's six p.m. right now. Your dad's had your car for how long now?"

"Eight hours."

"Text me in two hours if he isn't back. I'll get some guys to look around for your car."

I sighed. "Thank you. I love you."

"I love you. I'll call you later."

I was eating dinner – by myself on the couch – when my brother called.

"Hey. Where's Dad?"

"Heck if I know."

"What does that mean?"

"What do you think it means, Rafy?" I barked. "I don't know where Dad is."

"Where did he go?" my stupid brother asked.

"Dad is still gone, okay?"

"Have you called him?"

"I texted him and he said that he was sorry and that he'd be back as soon as he could."

"You know, that man of yours could probably get some of his guys to look for him."

"That man of mine is in the middle of real police work right now. I don't want him to bother looking for my truant father."

"I get that, too," Rafy grumbled.

"What did you need Dad for, anyway?"

"Wanda has to work late next Thursday, and there's a movie shooting in town. I want to do security for that."

Puerto Rico typically filled in as a filming location for foreign tropical movie productions. Rafy liked to volunteer to see behind-the-scenes stuff. I understood the appeal.

"What does that have to do with Dad? Do the boys have a game or something?"

"Two of them in one night. Mom can take them to one, but then she has a church thing. I wanted to see if Dad could fill in."

"I'm hoping to have Dad out of here by tomorrow evening, so I am going to go ahead and volunteer him."

"Works for me. Look; I got to go."

"Peace out," I said before disconnecting the call.

Esteban Morales rolled into my house at midnight.

"Oh. Did I keep you up?" he said as he walked into my apartment.

"What do you think?" I snapped at him.

Dad sighed. "I'm sorry."

"Sorry for what, Dad? You are going to have to be more specific."

"Getting caught up in stuff," he said as he let out a yawn. "I'm sorry. I'm beat. I am going to take a shower and tuck in, okay?"

Incredulous, I watched as my father set my keys down on the table and headed to my bedroom – where he closed the door behind him.

"Good night, beba." My dad called out.

I did not wish him the same. The next morning, Dad met me at the breakfast table, where I was drinking coffee.

“Did you sleep okay?” Dad asked as he poured himself a cup of coffee.

I slept okay, but that’s not what I said.

“What did you get into yesterday?”

“This and that,” Dad said as he shrugged. He then reached for my newspaper and began reading it.

“Dad,” I said, exasperation filling my voice.

“What?” he said, without lowering the paper.

Immediately, I had a new respect for my mother, whose temper could go from zero to sixty in five seconds. That was probably owed to a life lived with Esteban Morales.

“You aren’t being a good houseguest and you are not being the best father.”

That made him set the paper down. He let out a breath and tapped his fingertips to the table.

“I am sorry,” he said.

“Do you understand that an apology does not solve problems?”

Dad half-smiled at me. “How did you get to be so smart?”

“Caginess is what put you in a bad spot with me and Rafy. You said that you were done with that, but here you are, right back at it.”

“In my defense, I never said I was done being cagey. I said that I made a judgment call for my family that hurt them. I was sorry for that.”

I could not believe what my father was saying to me.

"Geographically speaking, you are closer to me now than you have been in a while. Emotionally speaking, though, you are putting in more distance."

"I'm sorry, Mija."

I shrugged. "You are who you are, I guess. But I am who I am. I need you to get on a plane tomorrow. My brother needs you, and I hope you can be there for him."

"Marta-" Dad called out as I got up from the table.

I shook my head and grabbed my bag. "No. I've got to go to work."

"Your first job isn't for another hour and a half. Sit down. Let's talk."

"No!" I snapped. "Yesterday was for talking! Last night was for talking! Today I have to get to work."

"Just sit and talk to me. Your cleaning schedule is right on your fridge. You don't have to be at Jane's for an hour and a half. You have no cleaning work to do."

"I never said I had cleaning work to do," I barked. I then took a breath and shook my head. "You had better not be late for my boyfriend, Dad. If you put Kevin out in any way whatsoever, I am going to call Mami and I am going to have her *fuck* up your life. Do you understand me?"

Dad let out another breath. "I understand."

"Fine. I'll see you later."

With that, I stormed out of my apartment and headed to my car. Once there, I noted the fast-food wrappers on my passenger seat, as well as my nearly empty gas tank.

I might have yelled some Spanish cuss words in my father's direction. But after that, I disposed my dad's trash and drove to a gas station. I had things to get to, anyway.

Chapter Eight

The night prior, Amanda had called me. So scared was she of my abandoning my case that she gave me her sister Becky's number, as well as scheduling a phone call appointment for me with Becky. Amanda had begged to be a part of the conversation, but I said no. When Amanda insisted, I told her I would quit. She backed off.

I drove to the lake and parked my car in a sunny spot. I gathered my pad and my pen and hit record on my recording device. After that, I called Becky.

"Hello, Becky. This is Marta Morales. Amanda should have told you that I would be calling right around now."

"Hi, Marta," Becky said with a sigh. "My sister said you would be calling me."

I noted reluctance and exasperation in Becky's tone.

"Is this a bad time, Becky, or is it just a bad subject?"

Becky laughed out loud, which was a relief to me. A happy, amused person was a more open person.

"It's both, I guess. I have to do some stuff at the hospital this evening, and I get the feeling it's going to be a late night. Also, my sister's fixation for Agustin Trujillo is pretty ridiculous."

Hmm. Becky Trujillo not only disregarded her father; she didn't think much of her sister just then.

"I get the feeling that you don't share your sister's enthusiasm for finding your father."

"You would be correct, Marta Morales. I barely have any memories of that man. I understand that my sister does, though, and some of those memories are good ones. He used to play the *cuatro* for her. He didn't do that for me, but that's probably because I was a baby."

My brow furrowed. "I'm sorry. Did you say that your father played the *cuatro*?"

"Yeah. The guitar?"

"I thought your father was Dominican."

Becky was quiet for a moment. "Um. Yeah. He was. I mean, I guess he is."

Amanda's sister was doing some backpedaling. What was she hiding?

"The cuatro is a Puerto Rican instrument."

Becky laughed. "You know, instruments do have a way of being played by all sorts of folks."

"Did your father spend time in Puerto Rico?"

"I don't know what my father got into. I don't know that man," Becky enunciated.

Crap. Becky was getting pissy with me. I had to get her to talk about something else before she hung up on me.

"Your sister said that your mother was a class act – that she never spoke ill of your father."

Becky let out a breath. "My mother was a saint. She never spoke badly of that man. Even though Agustin was a good-for-nothing leaver, my mother never disparaged him."

I had to put Amanda's name back into Becky's mouth. Becky would probably be less guarded if she was talking about someone else's emotions – and not her own.

"Amanda said that your mom thought that your father would return to you guys someday."

"I kind of remember my mom saying stuff like that. It meant more to Amanda than to me. My mother's brothers were more of a father figure to me than Agustin ever was."

"Aside from the abandonment, did your mother like your father?"

Becky let out a breath. "That's a good question. Um, my mother was young when she took up with Agustin. Agustin was a handsome Hispanic man. He played the guitar and could sing and dance. I think that was novel for my mother. I think that after he left and my mother got older, she kind of understood the gravity of what my father had done."

"Do you think she wanted him to come back?"

"In the beginning, I think she did. She felt shame that she'd been taken and abandoned like that. But…something happened when my sister turned seventeen and I turned fourteen."

"What's that?"

"I'm not exactly clear on that. I think that my mom had an altercation with some women out in town. They told her shit about my dad that she couldn't stomach."

"Do you know what was said? Do you know who said the things?"

"No, and no. Again, this was quite a few years ago. And also, my mom didn't take to talking bad about my dad in front of us. I only know about that altercation because I overheard her talking to my grandmother about it. And before you ask, my grandmother has passed away."

"Did your mother warn you to stay away from your father?"

"She did. She told us to stay away from him and quote-unquote his people."

I needed to wrap up the call, I knew.

"Why do you think your sister needs this so bad?"

"To find Agustin?"

"Yes."

"My sister is very smart. She's well-traveled and donates her time and money to charities and stuff. Aside from this, she is a great big sister. But I think she wants a family. I think that she thinks that she needs to resolve this before she can start her own family."

"But you don't need that, do you?"

Becky laughed. "I don't need something I never had. I don't want something back that was never there. Sure, if I can ever get my MD, get my residency done, and work enough hours to pay off my student debt, I *might* think about starting a family. I won't need to look back at some shit father to decide what would make a good father or husband."

"You've been very forthcoming, Becky," I lied. "One more question. What do you think I'll find when I find Agustin?"

"I think you'll find a drunk, broken old man shacked up with some woman. I think that when he learns that he has an I.T. professional and an MD as daughters, he'll want to come and play daddy again – with his hand outstretched the entire time."

"While strumming a cuatro?" I asked as I laughed.

"While playing a *seis* on a *cuatro*," Becky added as she laughed, too.

With that, I hung up the phone and hit the stop button on my recorder. I stared at the waves on Lake Michigan while I formulated my thoughts. Moments later, I hit record on my recording device.

"Becky knows more than she's saying. She thought she held everything back, but she revealed the fact that her father is probably at least half Puerto Rican. I don't know if that matters."

I mulled that over before speaking again.

"Becky probably knows where Agustin was last known to be. She at least knows more than Amanda. Becky is protective of Amanda, and is shielding Amanda from something."

I hit stop on my recorder and set it on my passenger seat. For a moment, I wished I could bounce ideas off my dad. But I wouldn't, as I was angry with him.

I looked at the clock and noted that it was seven-thirty a.m. Suddenly inspired, I bought some donuts and coffee and headed to my boyfriend's place of work, where I was sure I'd be welcomed.

Chapter Nine

I got through my residential cleanings and then my business ones. Filled with dread, I headed home.

Dad was there, as were wonderful aromas.

"What is this?" I said as I looked at the kitchen.

On the stove were a large pot of *arroz con gandules* (rice and pigeon peas), *guineos en escabeche* (wine and vinegar brined bananas), and *pernil* – roasted pig shoulder.

"I have some stuff to make up for, so, I catered some food and made others."

I couldn't help but smile. "You are still not out of trouble, but this helps."

Dad smiled and hugged me. "Here. Let me take your bag. Sit down and have a beer and food."

I laughed out loud. "Beer. Okay. You are mostly forgiven."

"I scheduled an appointment for tomorrow morning for your car to be detailed. I will also get the oil changed and will fill up your tank."

"The good news keeps coming!" I said as I laughed.

I said little as Dad and I stuffed our faces.

"What I will tell you about my ill-advised escapade yesterday is that I was taking care of business – old and new. I'm sorry that I took your time and your generosity for granted."

My good mood was replaced with a bit of anger. Apologies didn't solve problems. My father's problem was that he did what he wanted and expected his family members to deal with it. My problem was that I was mentally incapable of leaving stuff alone. If there was a puzzle, I had to finish it.

But my father was a puzzle that would probably never be solved.

With that in mind, I stared at my dad.

"Would you care for me to tell you how the meet with Kevin and the guys went?" He asked.

"Sure," I said.

Dad smiled. "They are fans. They know of Detective Connelly's work. They wanted to schedule him for an interview."

I smiled at my beer and nodded. "He's good at what he does."

"Not as good as you."

I chuckled. "Maybe not. But experience speaks for a lot. He's got far more years' experience than I."

"That is the truth. Now. What's in your investigation bag?"

I played the recording for my dad, as well as showing him my notepad.

"I have some time between appointments tomorrow," I said to him. "I found a Hispanic musical instrument store that borders Humboldt Park and Dominica. The hibachi restaurant where Agustin's Facebook image was purportedly tagged is in that area, too."

Dad nodded. "Not a bad idea to hit up traditional Hispanic music stores. You might get anecdotal data, but maybe not much on Agustin."

"I don't know. Agustin had a bunch of children – before Amanda and Becky, and most certainly after. Musical aptitude is inheritable. Who knows what the music store folks know?"

"Excellent points. Let's get back to Becky, though. That was an excellent catch on your part – the cuatro bit. You were canny in getting her to mention *seis* music. That is very specific."

I laughed. "Thanks. But it might not be a significant detail. It might be a distraction."

"True story. So, let's try to formulate what Becky knows, but won't share."

"Okay. Becky knows that her father is half Puerto Rican," I said.

Dad reached for a picture of Agustin.

"I can see that better, now that we know about the instrument stuff."

"This is what I think," I said as I reached for another portion of pork. "Becky realized – after discovering some unknown fact or facts – that her father was half Puerto Rican."

Dad's brow was furrowed as he stared at the picture.

"No. This man is completely Puerto Rican."

"What?" I said as I stood up from my chair.

I walked around to my dad's side of the table.

"Look at his cheekbones and his jawline."

"Crap. I see it."

I let out a breath and sat down at my place at the table again.

"Why would he hide his ethnicity?" Dad asked.

I thought about that for a moment before grabbing my laptop.

"Hold that thought," I said.

I went to Amanda's Facebook page, where I found all sorts of Dominican flags and Dominican pride graphics. I then went to Becky's page. There were some Hispanic Heritage graphics on there, but nothing that specified a particular ethnicity. I smiled and then turned the laptop screen to my dad.

"Becky knows she's half Puerto Rican. Amanda still thinks their dad is Dominican."

Dad smiled. "I think you're right."

I sighed and shifted on my chair. "It doesn't track that Becky caught onto this based on memories alone. Amanda's older than her and has more original memories of her father."

"Becky learned about her father's ethnicity after he left the family."

"Did their mother know?"

Dad thought about that for a moment before shaking his head. "I don't think so. If their mother was working hard to ensure that Amanda and Becky remember and respect their father's memory, she would have mentioned the fact that they were half Puerto Rican."

"Which means that their mother didn't know."

"Which means that Agustin Trujillo didn't want his partner or their daughters to know he was Puerto Rican."

"Agustin was hiding," I groaned. "Crap. Probably from Puerto Ricans in Chicago. Shit," I cussed.

Dad took his glasses off and dusted them on his shirt before putting them back on.

"Nineteen-eighties Chicago was a bad, bad scene."

"Dad? It still is."

"No. Not like back then."

I nodded. "Okay. Let's put a pin in that and get back to Becky. She somehow got a hold of information that told her what her ethnic background was. Or maybe a person?"

"DNA tests, probably," Dad said. "She's going to be a doctor. She probably did studies in genetics and thought to take a test."

"Or she met people with answers," I said.

"Do you still have access to that DNA test you did way back when?"

Just over a year ago, I'd done a DNA test as a way to research a sleuthing case I'd been working on.

Quickly, I logged into the DNA testing website. I typed in the name Rebecca Trujillo and saw her image there.

"Dang," I marveled.

Dad chuckled. "There she is."

"It won't tell me her DNA, though, and she isn't sharing her information publicly."

"She's hiding," Dad said. "That is smart."

I nodded. "Okay. Fine. So, Becky has genetic proof of hers and Amanda's background. Did Becky find a real-life link between the DNA test saying she's Puerto Rican and a real-life connection to her dad?"

"If she has, she probably won't tell you," Dad said. "You already got her to reveal far more than she meant to."

I was quiet for a while.

"I wonder if Becky hired her own P.I. Maybe found out stuff she thought was best hidden?" I posited to my father.

Dad nodded. "Very likely. Becky and Amanda's mother is gone. Judging from that phone call you had with Becky," Dad said as he pointed at the recorder, "Becky got the answers she wanted and moved on. She probably has a reason why she didn't share that information with her sister."

I groaned. "Amanda is romanticizing her father. Becky's probably protecting her." I thought about something for a moment. "Amanda did not want me to talk to her sister Becky."

"Why do you think that is?" Dad asked.

"I think that Amanda knows that Becky knows something. I think she wants to know what her sister knows, but is scared to learn it, too. If that makes sense."

"Of course it does," Dad said. "Amanda can live in a fantasy right now. The truth threatens the fantasy."

"I have to see this through, I think."

Dad nodded again. "Yes; you are still on the case. Unless you back out, that is. If you don't intend to quit the case, you owe your client some answers."

"I know," I said as I let out a breath. "This means that I am searching for a nineteen-seventies, nineteen-eighties Chicago-based Puerto Rican former gangbanger."

"That's not a good spot to be in, Mija," Dad said.

I didn't have an argument for that.

An hour later, Dad had the grace to spend time in my bedroom while Kevin came over to eat leftovers.

While Kevin ate (and drank my last beer), I presented to him what I'd learned about Agustin Trujillo.

"Fuck and fuck, Marta," Kevin cussed. "Please tell me I don't have to spell out what you already know."

"You don't. However, I do need a location for Agustin Trujillo. But I understand that I do not need to confront or even meet him."

"Because you have to understand that that man is dangerous, as well as everyone else he knows or is related to. That's not discounting his daughters in Milwaukee."

"You're not wrong."

Kevin nodded and then glanced at my barely-closed bedroom door. I smiled and blushed.

"What are you giggling for?" Kevin whispered. "I haven't even kissed your neck – yet."

I laughed out loud – only to hear my dad clearing his throat from my bedroom.

I rolled my eyes. "He leaves tomorrow afternoon."

Kevin half-smiled, and I blushed – again.

"When's the Ireland trip happening?"

Kevin let out a sad breath. "In a week and a half. It'll be for about four days."

"You need the break."

"Only from work. Not of you or anything else."

Soon after, I walked him to the door. After a long hug, he gave me a few kisses.

"Kevin's leaving," I called out to my dad.

Moments later, my dad was out there, shaking Kevin's hand.

"It's been a pleasure," he said.

"Likewise, Mr. Morales."

"Keep my guys posted. They will want to know what your plans are."

Kevin blushed. "I will. Fly safe, alright?"

"I will."

Kevin gave me a quick peck before telling me that he'd see me the following afternoon.

Dad and I watched the novela together that night – while Rafy and Mom listened via speaker phone. Ana Luz, the soap opera's protagonist, began to show a barely perceptible change in character.

"Oh, my goodness!" I yelled out loud. I'd just noticed that Ana Luz's apron pockets looked suspiciously heavy.

"What?" Rafy said. "What did I miss?"

"You didn't miss anything," Mom said. "We are watching the same thing."

"I figured it out," I said out loud.

Dad laughed but said nothing.

"What did you figure out?" my brother asked.

"Don't tell me – I don't want to know!" Mom called out.

I did anyway. "Ana Luz has been spending time with her two-timing boyfriend and her backstabbing best friend because she'd been copying all of their keys! She's a thief! Ana Luz is the bad guy!"

Dad laughed out loud while Rafy yelled over the phone.

"No!" Mom exclaimed. "No! Her boyfriend and her best friend betrayed her!"

Rafy laughed out loud. "Not as bad as she's going to get them," Rafy said. "Dang. I didn't see that coming."

"I did," Dad volunteered.

"When?" I asked him.

"The third episode. Ana Luz freaked out when she worried that her parking meter had gone over time. The amount of guilt and worry she felt was disparate from the crime itself. Ana Luz didn't want to be caught by any sort of authority figure."

"Wow," I said as I shook my head. "That is canny writing."

"Then who is the good guy?" Mom asked, panic filling her voice. "There has to be a good guy!"

"It ain't Ángel Alexis and it isn't her best friend," Rafy said.

"It's Ana Luz. We are meant to feel pity for her," Dad said.

"No," I argued. "Ana Luz is the greater deceiver. She never was a friend or a girlfriend. She was a thief. Thieves have no honor."

"True story," Rafy said. "Alright. I'm out."

"Why?" Mom exclaimed. "There's twenty minutes left on this episode."

"Because I know what happens. I think I'm going to try to catch a game," said Rafy. "Peace out."

I furrowed my brow a bit. "I'm sorry I ruined it."

"It's okay. We'll keep watching," Dad said. "The writing is still good. We won't see the reveal moment if we stop watching."

"This is it, though – the peak of excitement," I argued.

"Yeah, I was there two weeks ago," Dad agreed.

"What about me?" Mom whined. "Who will watch it with me?"

"I'm not going anywhere," Dad said. "I'll watch it with you now and when I get back, too."

Mom sighed. "Okay."

"I'm here, too, Mom," I added.

"You ruined it," Mom sighed.

"I'm sorry, Mom."

And I was. I needed to learn when to speak up and when to keep my mouth shut.

Chapter Ten

Dad's flight didn't leave until the late afternoon, so, he insisted on accompanying me to my cleaning jobs (after he'd taken the car to get detailed and got the oil changed and the gas tank filled).

Dad and Jamie – the pawn shop owner – got on very well. They talked about the Vietnam War, the economy, and everything Jamie had to sell. Dad looked at some of Jamie's vintage items and verified the authenticity of some items.

Barney's offerings mesmerized my dad. Barney showed my dad his finer wares, and some of his moderately priced ones, too.

Dad ended up buying shirts and slacks from Barney – with my discount.

"Bring your father back – anytime!" Barney called out to me as my father and I left.

"Nice people," Dad said as we drove back to my apartment.

I was sad as I watched Dad pack up his things.

"I didn't stay long enough," Dad said as he pushed his glasses up his nose.

I sighed. "Maybe not."

Dad looked around and touched one of the walls of my apartment. "This is a nice life you have, Marta. I like it."

"I like it, too."

Dad tilted his head. "No. I mean I like it for me. But, I can't, being that I have responsibilities in Puerto Rico."

"Mom, too," I said as I grabbed my purse.

"Yes, your mother, too. She's the only being who can scare me into walking the straight and narrow."

While we walked outside, Dad spoke again.

"But you can't stay here, Marta. This is temporary. You can't allow yourself to get addicted to the transient. You have a man who will want more one day. You have to be prepared to give that. You have a grandson who will demand more, soon. You can't give that here. You need to build for the future. This apartment does not allow for that."

I let out a breath as I turned my car on. "You're not wrong."

"You need to buy a house. Your mother and I are prepared to help you with the down payment."

"No, Dad!" I exclaimed.

"Yes, Marta," Dad asserted. "It's selfish, too, so you know we mean it."

"How do you mean?"

"Your mother and I would like a space of our own here in Chicago. If you get a house with a basement apartment, we could come and visit for extended periods. So: start looking, or I'll start looking for you."

That conversation was an interesting way to say goodbye to my father. We made it to O'Hare pretty quickly. Even with his ultimatum, I gave him a long hug and thanked him for his visit.

"Remember what I said about Agustin Trujillo. Old men and old gangbangers are dangerous because they are bored. They miss being relevant and respected. They miss power. If you confront Agustin, you will give him what he wants – power and access to his daughters."

I swallowed and nodded. "I understand, Dad."

He kissed the top of my head and then left for the security screening area. I let out a breath and then headed back to my car.

That night, Kevin came over with donuts – and an overnight bag.

"How are you?" he asked as he hugged me.

Not trusting my voice, I said nothing.

"I'm here," he said as he held me close.

Chapter Eleven

The next morning, Kevin shared his thoughts with me as we ate breakfast at my kitchen table.

"Oatmeal?" he said as he sighed.

"Yeah. We've been overdoing the bad carbs. We need to eat healthier because we are old," I said to him.

"Whatever. But that's not what I wanted to talk about. Your dad is trying to…ultimatum you into buying a house?"

I nodded and sat down at the table with my bowl of oatmeal. "I know. So, I need to buy a place soon – without a live-in basement."

"Those are hard to find."

"It's Chicago. Maybe I can find a place with a haunted basement."

Kevin nodded. "Not a bad plan, but I don't think that will put off Señor Morales."

"Yeah. Probably not. Now. Tell me how the meeting went with the feds!"

Kevin blushed and shrugged. "Well. It's nice to be liked. It's nice to be wanted."

I giggled. "I know."

"You more than like me or want me," he said in a voice that was a touch husky.

I laughed out loud. "Seriously. Are they wooing you?"

"They are trying."

"Are they getting somewhere?"

"Maybe. I don't know," he said as he sighed.

"Is there an 'us versus them' thing going on as far as city police and feds are concerned? A loyalty thing?"

Kevin sipped coffee before answering that.

"Loyalty – for sure. As far as the 'us versus them' thing is concerned, not as much as you would think."

"Will it get back to your captain – that the feds are interested in you?"

"Yeah."

"How do you feel about that?"

"I look forward to making him feel uncomfortable. Less than secure."

I nodded. "Maybe that will take the heat off your back?"

"Maybe. It is definitely food for thought."

We were quiet for a bit, which I was okay with.

"What are you getting into today?" Kevin asked.

"You mean beyond cleaning, don't you?"

"I do."

"First, I will meet with Ada to discuss HUD loan mortgages and applying – again. After that," I whispered into my coffee cup before taking a sip.

"What?" Kevin asked.

"I did some research this morning. I learned that there are a lot of Trujillos in Chicago that play the cuatro guitar. A lot of those guitar players talk about a musical instrument store by Dominica."

Kevin's blue eyes widened. "Not *El Bohío*. Tell me it's not that place."

I sighed. "It is."

"No, Marta. No. That place is a hangout for gangbangers."

"It's a very well-rated music store."

"Yeah! For musicians, which you are not. They are going to see you and know who you are, Marta."

"What's that?"

"Someone snooping."

He was so right that it pissed me off. I got up and walked to the coffee maker and poured myself another cup.

"Isn't there another way? There has to be another way," Kevin said.

I sighed. "Yeah. There is."

"What's that?" asked Kevin.

"Amanda's going to have to pony up some more cash."

"Why?" Kevin.

"I am going to buy a cuatro guitar."

Kevin wasn't happy with my compromise, but I thought it was pretty clever.

Amanda wasn't a fan, either.

"How much are you asking me to pony up here?"

"I'll need four hundred dollars additional to your deposit."

"For *what*?" she asked, sass filling her tone.

"I need to buy something from a particular store because that store will have information on your dad's whereabouts."

"Why not just go and ask? Why do you need to buy something?"

"It's a dangerous store in a dangerous area."

"You are street smart. You'll be fine."

"Don't be cavalier with my safety. And knock off the attitude," I snapped. "I understand you don't like the non-refundable expense. I'd rather you verbalize that instead of getting sassy."

Amanda took a loud breath. "I don't like that I am paying you an additional four hundred dollars for something that won't even be mine."

"That is a very reasonable concern."

"Thank you. Now, why do you need that guitar and why can't I have it myself?"

I sighed. "Are you sitting down?"

"Oh, shit. What are you going to drop on me? Yeah, I'm sitting down."

"Are you alone?"

I heard the sound of a door closing. "I closed my office door. Now, deliver some news to me that will make me feel good about shelling out three hundred dollars and giving you four hundred more."

"That was very assertive."

"Thank you. I am working on my boss-lady talents. I'm up for a big promotion where the boys won't want me to be."

"Keep that assertive tone of voice and keep speaking to me directly, like you are right now, and you'll be fine."

"Marta? What are you trying to tell me?"

"Amanda? You aren't half-Dominican. You are half Puerto Rican."

Amanda was quiet – but only for half a minute.

"What the fuck are you saying to me?"

"I have a strong suspicion that Becky knows that your father is – or was – Puerto Rican. I don't know how she attained that information, but it seems to be on point."

"My sister! Why didn't my sister tell me?"

I was saddened when I heard tears in her voice.

"I think that Becky was trying to protect you."

"Protect me? I'm the older sister! *I* do the protecting."

"I think that she is only concerned about you in this particular matter – in the search for Agustin Trujillo. Besides that, she is pretty proud of you."

"My head is spinning, Marta. Are you sure about this? About this Puerto Rican thing?"

I sighed. "Not entirely. But if I had to assign a percentage to it, I would say that I am about seventy-five percent sure."

"Oh, my goodness. Why didn't momma tell me?"

"Amanda, I don't know that your mother knew that about Agustin. But, if she did, I think that she, like Becky, was trying to protect you. Maybe you've built your parentage – and your father – into an ideal. Maybe your sister thought that that ideal was crucial to your identity."

"You don't understand, Marta! I have a Dominican flag tattooed on my back!"

I stifled a laugh by turning it into a cough.

"Don't you dare laugh at this, Marta!" Amanda said but chuckled as she said it.

"I don't mean to be casual about this. I am sorry."

"You aren't being casual," Amanda said as she groaned. "You just dropped a bunch of life-changing shit on me."

"You know, biologically speaking, Dominicans are a lot like Puerto Ricans."

"Don't sell me that shit! Puerto Ricans make fun of Dominicans all the time."

I said nothing, as I was embarrassed.

"It's not right – a lot of them jokes," she added.

"No, they aren't. But let me tell you, Hispanics aren't always the nicest of people."

"I know it," Amanda groaned. "I get so much shit from Hispanics because I am half black."

"Don't get me started on Puerto Rican men," I grumbled.

"I don't know what I am supposed to do with this information," Amanda said. "I mean, my sister knew. For how long? Did Momma tell her? Was it a DNA test? I haven't done DNA testing for a reason, Marta! I work in tech! I know how dangerous it is when companies have your DNA."

"You aren't wrong, Amanda. Your sister had her DNA tested. I don't know what came back on it, but you can probably rely on her results."

"But my sister didn't admit to you about the Puerto Rican thing."

"No, but she knew a lot of things about your dad that Puerto Ricans typically know. She's had some time to educate herself. Also, I had a subject-matter expert look at your dad's picture. He looks Puerto Rican."

"Jesus Christ. Wow. Boricua. Holy crap," Amanda said as she chuckled.

"About the money," I said. "I am going to buy a cuatro guitar. That will help ease me into the questions I need to ask."

"Come up to Illinois right now, and you'll get the money. No, you know what?"

"What?"

"I'll get you *eight* hundred dollars. You buy me a cuatro guitar, too. And a tablature book."

"A tablature book?"

"Yeah. Fingering for guitars. I'm teaching myself how to play the Ukulele. I ain't Hawaiian. If I'm Puerto Rican, I might as well teach myself to play the right kind of guitar."

I smiled. "Hey. Are you musically inclined?"

"Yeah. The only one in my family. My mom's brother played piano, but no one played the guitar."

"You got it from Agustin. According to your sister, he used to play the cuatro for you."

I heard sniffles on the phone, so I ended the call.

I was happy to meet Amanda at a café up north for the cash deposit.

"This feels sketchy," she whispered to me from across the table.

"I get why. I am unlicensed, though. It protects me, and my clients. I promise that I won't do you wrong."

Amanda rolled her eyes. "I don't know if this excursion has been worth it or not. Your findings have rocked my world."

I shrugged. "We can end this right now, and it might be for the best. I can give you half your deposit back and everything you just handed me."

"Nah. I'm all in now."

I nodded. "Okay."

"Tell me about something Puerto Rican that most state-bound Puerto Ricans don't know about."

"How about music?"

"I know everything there is to know about reggaeton, Marta."

"Not what I was going to say, Amanda. Don't assume," I gently reproved.

"My bad. What do you have for me?"

"Salsa music of the nineteen eighties. It was the best decade for that genre of music. I can text you the names of great Salsa singers."

Amanda nodded. "Okay. That sounds good. What else have you got?"

"Chances are that your father is descended from *Jibaros*."

"What are those?"

"Mountain folk – a cross between Spaniards, Native Americans, and African slaves."

"Uh – like Dominicans?"

"You and your attitude, young lady," I reproved. "You need to learn how to take in information without judgment."

Amanda blushed. "I'm sorry. You were saying?"

"Humility. At their core, Jibaros were humble. Even if poor, they shared. Even if scared, they smiled. They were kind – all the time."

Amanda smiled. "I like that."

I looked at my clock and nodded. "I've got to go. I will have more answers for you the day after tomorrow."

"I talked to Rebecca," Amanda said.

I eased back down into my seat. "How did that go?"

"Becky said a lot of what you said – how she was trying to protect me. I get the Agustin stuff. I just don't get why she kept it all to herself."

I thought about that for a bit. "Maybe it's hard for her, too. Maybe she doesn't have the energy or the vocabulary to get into the realization that what she thought she was, was something different than she actually is."

"'Didn't have the energy or vocabulary,'" Amanda parroted as she nodded. "I can see that."

"I remember my early twenties as being…difficult," I said. "I was a young mother in a bad marriage. But I also think that I would have been on edge anyway. A woman in her early twenties is never voluntarily vulnerable. Her emotions and her hormones are running the show. If a twenty-year-old woman is vulnerable, it is because her armor has been broken by someone else."

"Damn," Amanda said. "I felt that in my belly."

I laughed. "I'm twenty years past twenty, so I've had time to think about it."

"Yeah. With her studies, Becky is tired a lot, and on edge. So am I, for that matter. I have to be careful who I let in."

"I bet."

"I know you got to go, but did you hear about Awilda?"

I was going to speed to get home and back to Ana Luz and the rest of the novela, but a story about our shared friend Awilda would be more interesting.

"What's going on with Awilda?"

"She's moved to Puerto Rico with her kids. I don't get why. I hear the economy there is crap."

I sighed. "It is. But her family is there and her husband Arturo is not. I think she's tired of the military spouse life."

Amanda shrugged. "Her husband Arturo is hot – with all due respect," she added. "I bet that a guy like him won't stay single long."

"Wait. Do you think they are getting divorced?"

"Don't you? When a woman is willing to leave a country and a husband behind, she's ready to move on."

I sighed. "They loved each other. That's sad."

"Yeah. She might regret it one day."

"I agree with you. How sad is that?" I said.

After hearing those sad words, I left. Driving home, I wondered what Awilda's problem was. As I dozed off that night, I asked Kevin for his opinion.

"Maybe her problem is her pride. Maybe Awilda idealized a moment in her past. I don't know, so I can't say."

"Good night," I said as I yawned.

Kevin leaned over and kissed me again before wishing me a good night.

After my cleaning clients the next day, I headed to the guitar shop. The large room was carpeted and the walls were covered in wood. Strange-looking guitars adorned the walls. All sorts of cables and small speakers lined the floors, too.

"Can I help you?" said a young Hispanic-looking guy with long hair. He had an embroidered patch on his shirt that read "Santos."

I sighed. "Yeah. I'm in the market for a cuatro guitar."

The guy nodded. "You Puerto Rican?"

I nodded. "Yeah. It isn't for me; it's for my grandson," I suddenly decided.

Santos smiled. "That's great. Does he play the guitar already?"

I blushed. "Okay. He's only five and a half, but I have high hopes."

The young man laughed out loud. "Sure. Why not start him early?"

"Exactly."

"Follow me," he said as he motioned me towards a case near the back of the room.

I saw a nice cuatro guitar – for five hundred dollars.

"This here is a good model. But I'll tell you what. Maybe you or your…son should hang onto this until your grandson gets older," Santos said.

I shook my head. "It would be my daughter-in-law. My son passed away six years ago."

The guitar shop employee nodded. "Oh. Was he in the life?"

Wow. Kevin wasn't kidding about the gangbanger nature of the guitar store.

"Of a sort. A roadside bomb in Afghanistan."

"Wow. Sorry."

"Me too. But I have my grandson," I said as I half-smiled. "And maybe, with this cuatro, he'll have something of Puerto Rico in him – even in Chicago."

Santos cleared his throat a few times. "Yeah. Of course."

The salesman was nice, but it was time for me to lie a bit. "I learned about this store from a friend of mine in Milwaukee. Her dad used to be a cuatro player of some renown. He bailed on her family when she was a kid, though. She's teaching herself how to play guitar – in memory of him."

"Oh. Was he from here?"

I nodded. "Yeah. Agustin Trujillo was his name, I think."

I noticed Santos go very stiff. "Huh. That's a common last name. Can't say I know the name Agustin Trujillo, though."

I shrugged. "I guess. Look. Might you cut me a deal?"

"Deal. What kind of deal?" he asked. He was looking kind of cagey – and dangerous.

"I want two cuatros, but I only have eight hundred dollars."

The guy's eyes brightened. "A deal on *two* cuatros."

I nodded. "Yeah. My friend wants to learn how to play the cuatro and I want one for my grandson."

"What's your friend's name?"

Shit and shit.

"Mercedes," I lied.

"Yeah, I don't know her," Santos said.

"Well, she is from Wisconsin. But, do we have a deal? I can pay cash – not credit, if that makes a difference."

"It does," he said. "But if you sign up for our email program, I might be able to get you closer to your price."

Yeah, right. The guy wanted my name.

"Okay. I might be able to go over – slightly – if I can get a tablature book, too. If that's what it's called."

Santos laughed out loud. “Alright. Okay. Let me call my uncle to see if we can get a deal.”

I nodded and looked around at the stuff in his store. From the corner of my eye, I watched as the young man whispered into the phone a good bit. I suspected that he was asking his uncle about more than guitars, though. Five minutes later he came my way.

“Okay. So, the best I can do is eight-fifty. That will give you the cases and humidifiers, too.”

“Wait a minute. Humidifiers? The kind you plug into the wall?”

Santos laughed out loud. “No, not that kind. It’s these kind of gel packs you put into the guitar cases. You need temperature regulation to keep the wood in good condition.”

I sighed. “Okay. Alright. Eight fifty is fair.”

“Plus, your contact information for warranty stuff.”

Uh-oh. I couldn’t put up too much of a fuss. I didn’t want to raise any more flags than I already did.

“Okay.”

I gave Santos a fake name I could remember, and a number to one of my burner phones.

“What part of Puerto Rico are your people from?”

“Hatillo. It’s on the northwestern coast.” I did have family that lived in that town, so I wasn’t lying.

Santos. “Hatillo. Yeah, my people know about that place.”

"Are there any touring cuatro musicians here in Chicago?"

"Yeah. You can see them at the Puerto Rican pride festivals and stuff. If you go to the corkboard by the doorway, you'll see guys who teach the cuatro locally."

"Anyone in Wisconsin?"

Santos stopped filling out the receipt. He appeared to be lost in thought for a moment. "Maybe. Your friend might be better off finding someone up there on her own."

I laughed. "There isn't a Puerto Rican music scene anywhere in the U.S. like there is in Chicago."

The guy laughed out loud. "Quiet now. Don't let Jersey, Orlando, or New York hear that."

"Well, aside from awesome pizza, I think we are on the winning side."

Santos laughed out loud again. "You are funny."

I shrugged. "I do what I can. Do you mind if I take a picture of the corkboard before I go?"

"Sure thing."

I smiled as the man stacked the guitar cases on the counter. I even laughed and clapped, which made him laugh.

"Are you sure you don't want the lessons?"

I shook my head. "No. This dog is too old to learn new tricks. Mercedes is younger, though, and willing to learn."

"Let me help you load these in your car."

"Sure thing," I said.

Back in my trunk, I shoved cleaners around.

"You like cleaning?"

"I do what I can to make ends meet," I hedged.

"I understand that."

I furrowed my brow and stared at the young man. "Are you sure that putting those guitar cases in my trunk is good for the cuatros? I don't want my cleaning fumes to…do stuff to the wood and stuff."

Santos laughed out loud. "I think you're okay. Your chemicals are in bins and these cases are pretty hard," he said as he tapped the guitar case.

The young man stood up and stared at me. "Are you a cop?"

I blinked a few times. "Once upon a time."

The salesman shook his head. "Lady, you don't want to be here if you are a cop. Don't come back. I tell you that because I think you are alright."

I sighed. "Okay. I'll be straight with you. Save for names, I have told you no lies. My son died in the war. I want this for my grandson, and my friend wants this cuatro because she wants to learn how to play."

"I believe you. But I also know you can buy cuatros in Wisconsin."

"Yeah, but I can't find out what happened to Agustin Trujillo up that way."

The salesman let out a breath. “Man, you don’t want to throw that name around here. There are lots of dangerous Trujillos out this way.”

“Can you tell me one thing?”

“Man; I’ve told you enough. You need to go,” he asserted.

“Just one thing and I’ll leave you an awesome review on Yelp – which you’ve merited.”

Santos laughed out loud. “Make it Facebook and Google and I’ll consider it.”

“Agustin Trujillo – is he dead? Are his sons the dangerous ones now? I want nothing to do with them, by the way. I just want to tell my friend to leave shit alone.”

The guitar salesman’s face fell. “All of his family were – and are – in the life. If he left bastards in Wisconsin that weren’t in the life, then they are better off.”

I gave a slow nod.

“Your friend? So-called Mercedes? Her mother’s black, isn’t she?”

Shit and shit and shit.

“She’s passed away, but yes.”

The salesman looked out at the road. “My uncle heard of Agustin’s wife. She never said bad shit about Agustin. That meant something to Agustin. Tell you what: I’ll give you a name.”

“Okay,” I said as I nodded.

"Sister Lucia Trujillo."

"Who is that?"

"A nun. One of Agustin's kids. She's up in Eau Claire, Wisconsin. A convent. She's trying to atone for all the shit Agustin did."

"Wow," I said.

"I know. Between you and me? She'll probably have to pray rosaries for the rest of her life."

I nodded. "Thank you, Santos."

"Thank you for your business. I like your money, but don't come back here."

I blushed. "I understand."

I got on the road and made a quick call to my father.

"Hey, Mija. Miss me?"

I laughed. "I do. I found a resolution to the Agustin Trujillo case."

"Tell me about it."

So, I did.

"Dad. Did you look into Agustin Trujillo while you were here?"

"I did."

"Is he dead?"

"Yeah. Heart attack. It was too kind a death for him."

"I'm glad you didn't tell me," I said.

"I know. You like to find your way. I like your resolution better, too."

With that, I hung up with him. After that, I called Kevin.

"How'd it go?" he asked.

"A combination of how I thought it would go and how you thought it would go."

Kevin cussed under his breath. "I knew that you left the store okay. There was a car on the cross street watching out for you."

I let out a breath. "You put a lot of resources into watching out for me."

"Whatever. It was nothing."

"I have to go home and do some research before I drive north to meet up with Amanda. I'll call you later."

"Okay. Love you."

"You too."

Two hours later held me meeting with Amanda at a café by her place of work.

She clapped and laughed as she accepted the cuatro guitar case from me.

"God. Jesus. Why am I crying?" she asked as she dried her eyes.

I laughed and handed her a tissue from my purse.

"Try it out. Let your music speak to us first."

"Damn. That's well said."

Amanda grabbed the guitar, twisted the tuners around, and then strummed some strings.

"This is speaking to me," she said as she held the guitar.

"What's it saying?"

"It's telling me that sometimes answers don't come in word form."

I nodded. "Well, I have some word-form answers if you want them."

"I'll take those, though," she said as she laughed and placed the cuatro back into its case.

Instead, I handed her a two-sided printout of what I'd found out about Agustin Trujillo – from beginning to end. I watched as Amanda quickly ready through my report.

"He's dead?" Amanda said as she turned to me.

"Yeah. And, I looked up the Trujillo family members. Three separate Trujillo names and numbers were on a corkboard at the guitar shop. I don't know how directly related they are to Agustin, but…at least two of them have a history with the cops. I am sorry that I don't have better news for you."

"Me, too. I'm not going to get the answers I want."

"Let's try something. Why don't you ask me the questions? I'll pretend that I can answer for him."

Amanda shrugged. "Okay. Didn't my father love us?"

"He had lots of kids," I said as I shrugged. "He didn't want anything bad to happen to any of them, but he had other stuff he wanted to do."

"Did he think about us?"

"Yeah. He thought fondly of your mother. But as far as parenting was concerned, Agustin's dad probably wasn't around, either. He probably had no good father figure. So, he felt no guilt over what he did or didn't do."

"Shit. That sounds about right."

"It sounds like he kept feelers out for you guys."

"He wasn't there when Mom got beat up at the salon where she worked. Wasn't there when I was assaulted in high school. He wasn't fucking there. Shit. He lied and let us think we were Dominican."

Amanda was finally angry. I was glad to see it. Still, I wanted to help her keep her tenderness alive. "Maybe he lied to protect you guys, too."

"I think it was more out of self-preservation than anything else."

"There's that nun's name there. You can try to reach her."

Amanda shrugged. "She's probably in contact with folks from before. I don't think I need her connecting me to them. The last thing I need are thug half-brothers looking for a handout."

"Are you mad at your sister?"

"Nah; Becky did the best she could with what she knew."

"How about your mom?"

Amanda let out a breath before answering that. "How do you get mad at a saint?"

"What do our parents owe us?" I mused.

"My dad gave me life. That was about it."

"True. But, do they owe us honesty?"

"I don't know. What I do know is that I have answers. Because of you. I think I can move on now."

"Are you in a better spot?"

"No, but I'm in a different spot and that means something. I got a tattoo on my back that means nothing. But I can get it covered."

"Or you can get it removed."

"Yeah. Do you not like tattoos?"

I shook my head. "No. Those got big after my generation. But I don't like them. A permanent mark on your body does not let you change your story. I mean, it doesn't mean that that mark doesn't mean anything anymore. I just think that maybe a tattoo will lose its meaning. It will present a part of your life that you might not want to share."

"Damn, Marta. Your philosophy is almost too heavy. Is that a Puerto Rican thing?"

I laughed out loud. "It might just be an older person thing. Bullshit might be a Puerto Rican thing. Beware of Puerto Rican salesmen."

"Wish someone would have warned my mother."

"I want to hear you make music, okay?"

Amanda nodded a few times. "Yeah, of course."

"Seriously; cuatro guitar playing is nearly a lost art. Perhaps that's something you can bring back."

"Fuck, Marta. Quit trying to make me cry," she said as she wiped the corners of her eyes.

I laughed out loud. "Okay. I will leave you now. You know where to find me, okay?"

Amanda surprised me by hugging me. "I do. Thank you."

"You are welcome."

That night, I told Kevin what had gone down with Amanda.

"I hate that you gave me intel on the Trujillos that I cannot share," Kevin said as he rubbed deodorant under his arms.

"Well, you can use it personally, but no – you cannot share it with others."

"That's fair, I guess. Your dad's right, Marta. You gave Amanda a neat, bow-tied resolution."

I shrugged. "I guess. I never figured out who was in that Hibachi restaurant picture, though."

"Investigative work is not like the movies," he said as he pulled a white t-shirt on. "We don't get answers to all of our questions."

"The answers are not worth our safety," I added.

"Amen to that," Kevin said before climbing into bed and turning off the lamp.

Chapter Twelve

The novela *¿Quién Ama a Ana Luz?* was not over. The soap opera was so well received it was that the Puerto Rican production company that owned the novela tacked another month onto it.

The drama that was going on in my life persisted, too.

I was in a good place, though. Kevin and I had gotten *very* comfortable with each other, I'd solved Amanda's case, Dad and I were doing better, and I'd reapplied for a HUD mortgage loan.

But, like the plot twists that kept the soap opera interesting, my life was about to take another surprising twist.

I'd just finished cleaning my kitchen and bathroom when my phone rang - my private investigator phone.

"Huh," I muttered. "I hope Amanda's still okay."

I hit the green answer button on my phone. "This is Marta."

"Hey!" The loud, gravelly voice said. "Remember me?"

How could I forget the deep, foul-mouthed voice of José Villanueva? I'd 'met' him a couple of months back while trying to find the voluntarily disappeared Cassidy Russo. José had been of help - as painful as it was to talk to him.

"José Villanueva," I said to the landscaper.

"Hey! You said my last name right. I didn't know if you spoke Spanish, or if you were some sort of young, lazy

Hispanic punk who didn't feel the need to know their motherfucking mother language."

I had never heard the words 'motherfucking mother' being said together, and I marveled at that. I lived in Chicago, after all. I wondered if Kevin had heard those words put together. Probably, I mused. Instead of going down that rabbit hole of thought, I said something else.

"If those punks grew up hearing English spoken in their homes, English would be their mother language."

"Bullshit! What are the odds?" José argued.

"Pretty good. I cannot speak to all Hispanic cultures, but I can tell you that as far as Puerto Ricans are concerned, my generation's grandparents started making that move. The economy in pre-1950 Puerto Rico was very, very rough, which caused the initial diaspora. Hurricanes, religion, and cultural norms made for a scarcity of food and a surplus of babies."

"Excuse the fuck out of me. Spouting education shit and stuff."

"I'm offending *you*?" I said, starting to get pissy. "You talk like a truck driver. In my attempts to try to shed some light on some Hispanic migrations, I offend *you*?"

"I'm glad you didn't say I cuss like a sailor. Let me tell you, those motherfuckers can cuss like no one else. I'm a Marine, though." José let out a breath. "I got some rough edges - I know that. They fit my life in the military, though, and they sure as fuck come in handy when dealing with the ex-cons who work my landscaping business."

I nodded. “I saw your website and noticed who you employed. That’s commendable work you are doing.”

“I think so. But the truth is that those ex-cons work harder for me than lazy fucking young adults living in their parent’s basements. This generation’s entitled brats don’t have the work ethic their parents do - sure as hell don’t have the ethics their grandparents did.”

The conversation with José was going a lot longer than I thought it would. I went over to the fridge and got myself a bottle of water.

“Let me try to peg you. You talk angrily and loudly. Are you at least half Cuban?”

José laughed out loud. “You got me. The other half is Dominican, which is why I am so friendly and gregarious.”

That made me smile.

“I pegged you as Puerto Rican,” José Villanueva continued. “You sound like you are snooty and educated and shit. Do you think like the other Puerto Ricans - that you are better because you are born a citizen?”

His tone was teasing.

I shook my head. “No. I think I’m better because I know what I am talking about when I throw statistics out there. Also, because I don’t cuss.”

That made José laugh. “You got a man?” he asked of me.

I shook my head. “Put your Dominican charm away.”

“Was it working?”

“It’s more amusing than it is effective.”

"Huh. I am going to have to think about that."

I sipped water while I waited for José to get to the point of his phone call.

"You didn't answer my question about having a man."

"You're right. I didn't. Why are you calling me, José Villanueva?" I said before sipping water.

"Right, right," he said. "Private investigators like you are busy. So. Did I tell you that I am pretty good at investigating, too?"

"It didn't come up."

"I am. When I hire ex-cons, I have to determine if they are on the straight-and-narrow, or if they are fucking around until they get locked up again."

I sat down on a chair, as the conversation with José was starting to get interesting.

"That's good thinking. How do you do that?"

"By fucking following them. Seeing where they hang out. Seeing where they live. Checking out to see if they meet with their parole officers. I verify that they go to their therapy meetings. I try to tell if they are paying their child support and shit. If that crap checks out, they land a job with me. I'm as mean as their prison guards were and worse than a drill sergeant. The ones that stick around get a good paycheck, health and dental, and even a 401K."

"Wow," I said. I was so impressed I could not say more.

"Yeah. You got to put pride in your work, or you'll put shit work out there. That's what I'm trying to teach my knuckleheaded son."

"I hope it takes."

"You and me both."

I stared at my dry-erase board, which noted the cleaning jobs I had to do, as well as Kevin's upcoming Ireland vacation.

"This has been a very interesting phone call, José, but...was there a point to your call?"

I was polite when I asked the question, and chased it with a sip of water, as I guessed that José Villanueva would have a very verbose answer for me.

"I found Cassidy Russo's baby daddy."

Instead of providing an articulate, educated answer, I spat water onto my freshly-wiped refrigerator.

Chapter Thirteen

I wiped my face and then glanced at my phone.

"I'm sorry. Did you say you found Cassidy Russo's baby's father?" I said, incredulity filling my voice.

Cassidy Russo was the 'voluntarily missing woman' case I'd worked on a few months back. I'd found her by calling all of her stupid cell phone numbers – all nine of them. José Villanueva owned one of those old cell phone numbers, which was how I'd had the fortune to meet him.

My case had NOT been to find Cassidy Russo's baby daddy, although I would have welcomed that opportunity had it been offered. Owed to the nature of Cassidy Russo's lifestyle, Charity Russo – Cassidy's daughter – was now in foster care waiting for my friend – Angie Bonacci – to adopt her.

"I did," José proudly said.

I got up from my dining chair and paced.

"You've left me at a loss for words, José. I'm not trying to brag here, but that doesn't happen much."

"Glad it was me."

His voice had a leer in it when he said it. I ignored that.

"If I had been hired to undertake that tasking, it would have been HARD," I asserted. "Even knowing all I did. You knew less than I did. How did you pull that off?"

"Like I said, I do investigating shit. It comes easy to me, but...I scare folks off with my looks. Works sometimes.

Sucks others. Anyway, you weren't the only person calling me looking for Cassidy Fucking Russo. Her mom had called me as did other assholes such as creditors and shit. One creditor was a guy who ran a chain of salons in Ontario, Canada. Apparently, Cassidy owed that stupid fucker some money, too. I remembered what you said about the baby daddy being in Canada and shit. I figured that Cassidy wasn't going to Canada a lot so that one visit was probably her only one. So, using the dates left to me by the polite Canadian salon owner, I researched hotels in that area. I learned that there had been a hairstylist convention up there during the time Cassidy visited our neighbors to the north. I even found the hotel where the convention was held, and where she probably stayed."

"I have GOT to stop and give you props on all of that. I mean, I can't wait to hear the rest, but...wow."

"Yeah, thanks. So... I call the guy who runs the restaurant at that hotel. I asked him if he worked there four years ago. He did. I then told him about what was about to happen to Cassidy's daughter. I implored him to help me find the guy Cassidy spent time with. He's balking, because, shit; why would he go along with my scheme? So, I gave him time. Gave him my phone number, my website, and even the number to my best friend, who is still in the Marines."

"So. A week after I made the first call, the restaurant manager called me back and said he was going to help me out. Turns out he's Russian Orthodox and very much into the preservation of the family and shit. So, this guy is clever, too. He pulls up the transaction record he has for the nights of the convention. So, Cassidy only paid for one drink with her credit card - but she was there for four hours!"

"Who would that surprise?" I said with a sigh.

Cassidy was a beautiful young woman, but one who took the easy way out of everything.

"Only a fucking idiot would fall for that shit. But guess what?"

I sat down on my chair again, as I was riveted by José's testimony.

"What?"

"I got the name of *the* fucking idiot. The restaurant manager spoke to the bartender on duty who still worked the hotel restaurant bar. The bartender said that if he looked at the credit card receipts and signatures, he could probably remember the guy. And he did."

I stood up and paced. "Oh, my goodness. Oh, my goodness! Wow!"

José laughed. "That's what I said. But with more cuss words."

"You said you found him. How is that going? Does he remember Cassidy? Does he believe that he got her pregnant and that he has a daughter in Chicago who is in the system?"

"Yeah. So, check this shit out."

I didn't know if my heart could handle any more intrigue. The stuff José was telling me was more dramatic than the *¿Quién Ama a Ana Luz*? telenovela.

I nervously shook my foot under the table while I awaited José's latest bomb.

"He's here in Chicago. His name is Raymond Danskin and he's ready to meet his daughter and do whatever he has to do to get custody of her."

"Sweet. Lord. Almighty."

"No, shit," said José. "Want to meet up with me and him?"

Did I ever.

Chapter Fourteen

Once in my car, I made a quick call to Kevin, which went straight to his voicemail.

"Hey. I know you are busy, but I wanted to tell you that I have to go to the other side of town to meet with a guy about a thing. It has to do with an old case. Love you and talk to you later."

I kept my radio off while I drove, as I had to think some things out loud.

"Okay," I said to myself. "Alright. The facts. What am I doing? I am driving to the other side of town to meet with José. Why? I am meeting with him to determine whether or not I am going to divulge what I know about little Charity. Who? I'll be meeting with José. Raymond Danskin is the purported father of Charity. He'd better not be there. Why? Okay, it appears that José has a flair for drama. I should consider the fact that Raymond might be there. What do I want to know? I want to know if this dad is for real and if Charity's best interests lie with him."

I stopped talking out loud for a while. I was forgetting something - I knew it. When it came to me, I reached for my phone and dialed a number.

"Hey. What are you up to?" my friend Angie asked.

"I am hoping to make it out to see you late this afternoon, or early this evening. Will you still be at your store?"

Angie let out a groan. "Yeah. I decided to rent out my backroom as a place for LARPers to plan a thing and as a space for RPG players."

"Is it weird that I know exactly what you are talking about?"

Angie laughed. "Yeah, but that stuff was popular when we were young, so..."

"Live-Action-Roleplay? That is so not a Gen X thing."

"Right?" She said as she laughed. "Dressing up and pretending you are in a role-playing game? That's a bridge too far."

I laughed, too. "Those kids need to get into other things."

"No doubt. Teenaged pregnancy, gangs, and drugs are other viable outlets," she whispered on the phone.

"Hey! You are supposed to be a school psychologist," I teased.

"I know!" Angie said as she groaned. "I might have to get back at that here soon."

I was waiting to hear what else Angie had to say, but that would have to wait, as she started yelling at someone about spray paint on her conference tables.

"That is coming out of the deposit!" she yelled. "Come on, you guys! Aren't you supposed to be in college?" There was a commotion on the phone. "Look, Marta; I have to go. Come on over later and we'll talk, okay?"

"Yeah. For sure."

I was going to say something else, but the dial tone dispelled that. I set my phone down, but it rang again. I picked it up as I knew the number by heart.

"Where, when, who and why?" asked Kevin.

I sighed. "Aren't you busy with work stuff?"

"Yeah, but not busy enough to find out what you are getting into."

I groaned. "It's so long a story and I am almost there. Can we get into it later?"

"You just solved the Amanda/Agustin Trujillo case. Why are you getting into something else?"

"It's not my case - yet. Look - I'm about to text you the name of the restaurant I'm going to along with the name of the guy I'm meeting, okay?"

"I don't like this."

"I understand. But it will be okay. I promise I'll bring you up to speed later."

Kevin grumbled a reply I couldn't make out.

"I love you," I replied.

"And I love you. But if you get hurt or get in trouble, I am going to be pissed off."

"Understood. Hanging up so I can text you."

So, I hung up and texted Kevin the information I'd promised him. Once that was done, I got back on the road.

Five minutes later held me parked outside of an establishment I'd never heard of. It looked dark on the outside and it probably looked the same way on the inside. I was sorry that I was going in alone.

I pulled my phone out and called José.

"This place is skeevy looking. Why are we here and not at a more up-and-up-looking place?"

"Yeah - this place looks fucking skeevy, but the food is top-notch."

"I'm not here for dinner; I am here for a meeting."

"The owner is a former police officer, okay?"

"Retired or fired?"

José sighed. "Good question, being where we live and the times we are living in. He's retired, okay?"

"Forced or voluntary?"

"Fuck, Marta! Voluntary."

"Alright. I'll be in in a minute."

Still, I checked my purse for my pepper spray and found it, along with my mini recorder and my cell phones. Thinking quickly, I hit record on my mini recorder and then walked into the restaurant.

The locale was quite nice on the inside. White oak floors looked stunning against maroon-painted walls, which were adorned with pictures of vintage Chicago. A well-dressed greeter stood behind a podium at the entrance.

"Good afternoon," she said as she smiled at me.

"Hello. I'm here to meet-"

"She's here with me, Darla," called out a voice from the back of the room.

I looked that way and saw a buff, medium-height, shave-headed, tattooed, Hispanic man. I recognized him from the website and I gave him a half smile.

"I am here to meet him," I said to her.

"Then follow me."

José was not alone, though. An older man wearing a white shirt and khaki slacks leaned on a wall while he talked to José.

"You must be Marta," said the man who was unmistakably a former police officer.

I nodded. "I am."

"Mikey, this is Marta Morales - the lady who knows something about the thing I am looking into. Marta Morales, this is retired detective Michael Nolte."

I shook his hand. "It's nice to meet you."

"At your service," said the nearly white-haired man as he shook my hand back.

Mikey shoved off from the wall. "Let me bring you some drinks and some of our freshly baked olive garlic bread."

I sighed. "I wasn't even hungry, but how can I say no to that?"

"You can't," Mikey said as he smiled. "I'll be right back."

Mikey left, leaving José and me at the table.

"You look like I thought you would," he said to me.

I laughed out loud. "I don't know what to say to that, but okay."

"You had me at a disadvantage. You can see me on my website. I didn't know what you looked like."

"That's what happens when you make yourself public," I said to him before opening my menu.

José grunted. "Shit. I know it. However, for my sake, face recognition helps with my brand recognition. People know what they get with me. That's bankable."

"Fair points," I said as I looked at the menu.

"What about you? What do you do?"

I looked up from the menu. "This and that."

"Fuck that. I need more."

I sighed. "I'm a housekeeper."

"I couldn't find a website on you, only cleaning reviews. And let me tell you, they weren't that great."

I let out a low, slow breath. "Those reviews had nothing to do with my housekeeping and everything to do with old business gone bad."

"Yeah?" he asked as he sat back.

I sat back, too. José was a straight-up guy, so I thought I'd give him more. "I do extra stuff outside of housekeeping. I don't talk about that work with anyone outside of my circle."

"Put me in that circle. I can help you out."

"I don't even know you."

"Yes, you do," José said as he scoffed.

Just then, Darla - the server - brought us bread, olive oil, and some wine.

"Mikey's decided to go ahead and choose your meal. You won't be disappointed."

"Thanks, Darla," José said to her.

After she left, I stared at José a bit.

"You aren't a one-face man - no matter how much you try to sell that."

José lost some of his humor. "How do you mean?"

"I'm not speaking a foreign language to you, José," I said as I sipped my red wine. Damn. It was good. "It isn't fair of me to try to read you like that. Let me backpedal a bit and tell you why I don't plaster my face all over the place."

José looked reserved but open to what I had to say.

"I have cleaning clients that are loyal to me, and I to them. So, as far as that front is concerned, I'll always have work there. As far as other things are concerned, being anonymous and overlooked is key."

"But you are attractive. Especially your body. Don't get me wrong," he quickly interjected. "I'm not hitting on you - unless you want that," he coyly added.

"I don't," I said as I sipped my water.

"My point is that you aren't as overlooked as you think."

New enemies and old ones came to mind. Maybe Agustin Trujillo's kin. Maybe Niels Ericsson – a rich, brilliant dangerous man I helped a friend escape from. While that friend might have forgotten about me, I wasn't so sure that Niels had.

"You aren't wrong. When I get too familiar with clients, they stare a bit longer. I can't afford that, so, aside from my regulars, I am pretty aloof with everyone else. I need to be forgettable because it helps me in my other work."

A few minutes later wonderful pasta dishes were delivered to our table.

"Wow and wow," I said as I beamed at Mikey.

Mikey laughed. "Thank you. You'll love it."

"I love it already," I sincerely said.

A few bites later had me forgetting about an Italian restaurant chain I'd previously been in love with.

"You know shit you didn't learn housekeeping. Where'd you learn it?" José asked me.

I finished my mouthful and then pointed my fork at José. "I'm not giving you my life story, José. I will share a bit more before we get down to business, though."

"Fair," he said as he had a swig of wine.

"I used to be a cop. That was a long time ago. I don't talk about where, when, or why."

"Shit," José said to me.

I shook my head. "Not important. That was a long time ago. I picked up other stuff before and after. I still do."

"Never stop learning. That's what my dad taught me. He was rough in his youth. Made mistakes that courts couldn't forgive. Turned around anyway, though. Went to church, started a family, and a business that was all about hard work and second chances. The Marines don't forgive fuck-ups. I didn't fuck up during my time, but I saw others mess shit up. I had a problem with that. I did my time and started a business that was about the forgiveness that my dad was all about."

I smiled. "Your father sounds like a remarkable man."

"He was. Trusted the wrong guy, though. Took him out during an electrical job. Stole his tools and his truck to get money for drugs. It took me a while to forgive that fucker, but I did. He's in jail forever, but works hard to teach the young punks in there to turn their shit around."

"I am sorry for your loss, José. Your father might need to be canonized."

José laughed out loud. "Nah. He cussed too much."

I laughed, too. Soon, we finished our meals.

"Alright, here's the deal," José said as he looked at his watch. "I had you here early to figure you out. Can't say I did that, but I will say that I have a good gut feeling about you."

"That's fair," I said.

"Let's go to the bar. That's where the Canuck is supposed to meet us - fifteen minutes from now."

I nodded. "Well planned."

"Thank you."

I reached for my wallet, but José quickly rejected that. "Don't insult me."

I groaned. "Alright. Thank you, Sir," I said to him.

"Fuck. That is some polite shit."

Before joining José at the bar, I went to the ladies' room, where I used the facilities, touched up my makeup, and checked my mini-recorder. It still had a good bit of juice in it.

"Let's go," I said to myself.

I met José at a small round table in the bar area of the restaurant. I opted for a cup of coffee instead of another glass of wine. José ordered a diet soda himself.

We said little, and I was okay with it. Perhaps José was getting his game face on. I did the same. I would evaluate Raymond Danskin as well as José Villanueva. Five minutes after getting our drinks, a tall, red-headed man entered the restaurant.

I stared at him - hard. I compared his face to my mental image of Charity's. They didn't look different, but I couldn't immediately peg her as his daughter. Babies faces changed a lot, though.

"Mr. Danskin," José said as he stood up and waved to the man.

The man blushed, smiled, and came our way.

"Hello. Sorry, I'm late."

"What are you talking about?" José said as he smiled and extended a hand in greeting. "You are right on time."

"Nice to meet you in person, Mr. Villanueva."

I stood up and extended my hand. "My name is Marta, Mr. Danskin."

The man shook my hand and blushed. "A pleasure to meet you, Ma'am."

I laughed. "I'm being called Ma'am. Well. I guess we've got to age one day."

"Shut up, you," José said as we all sat down. "I'm waiting to switch on the charm. You just let me know."

I groaned and rolled my eyes before turning back to Raymond Danskin.

"Mr. Danskin. Is this your first time in Chicago?"

"I meant no offense in calling you ma'am," said Mr. Danskin. "I guess I am being overly polite. I am guilty of being Canadian that way."

"No offense taken. How's your trip going?"

"I've not been this way before. I usually stay home in Canada. I make it to Vermont from time to time. Have you been?"

I nodded. "I have. I'm from New England originally."

"You didn't mention that," José said.

No, I had not. My Boston accent only came out when I was into my drinks.

"How do you two know each other?" Raymond asked of us while politely smiling at the waitress.

"Met through a work thing," said José. "We're colleagues of a sort."

Raymond ordered a beer and had a few swallows.

"I hate being rude, but I don't have much time. I have to get back to my work in Canada. I want my daughter. Yesterday."

The abrupt change of subject was jarring, but welcome.

"Straight to the point," José said. "I like that."

"Of course. I did not know that Cassidy had become pregnant," he said, steel lacing his tone. "Had she told me, I would have done right by her. Child support, whatever. Hearing that she had my baby and is living a lifestyle that is leaving my daughter in a dangerous situation infuriates me. I've hired an attorney back home. I'm ready to fight the courts - anyone - to get my daughter."

José nodded. "That kind of passion is good to see. Determining that you are in fact Charity's father will help speed things up."

"A DNA test. Blood, spit, whatever. I am ready to provide that," Raymond added.

José looked at me and then at Raymond.

"Marta here is the live link to Charity and Cassidy, Raymond."

“I thought you had Cassidy’s number,” Raymond angrily said.

“I know how to find her.”

“Not the same thing,” Raymond rebutted.

“No shit,” José said, his spikes coming up a bit.

Time for me to interject.

“Cassidy is in a delicate situation, Mr. Danskin,” I gently said.

“Even more of a reason to get this show on the road,” he angrily replied.

“I know who Charity Russo is. I know who Cassidy Russo is. I don’t know you from Adam,” I said, starting to get pissy myself.

“What else do I need to say? What else do I need to give you? Here,” he said as he reached for his pocket.

For a moment, I was worried that he would be pulling a gun out. Instead, he dropped his wallet there as well as his passport.

“Birth Certificate. I’ll provide my social insurance number. You can do a background check - whatever you need to do.”

“The burden of proof is not on us,” I said. “It is on you. José did you - and Charity - a service. If you are Charity’s father and are trustworthy,” please forgive me, Angie, I mentally added, “then she belongs with you and we will aid you in attaining custody of her.”

"I am trustworthy. I've worked hard every day of my life," Raymond said as he pointed at the table with his index finger. "I am a good man. I am worthy of trust."

"You are a foreigner," José said.

"As is my daughter! Pardon my crass tongue, but not only is she half Canadian, she was conceived there."

"Perhaps you are trustworthy," I said. "But are those you trust trustworthy?"

Raymond let out a breath and sat back on his chair. He rubbed at his forehead and then had a long swallow of beer. He was about to say something, but his phone rang. He let out a breath.

"Pardon me. I have to get this."

I was surprised when I heard him speak French on the phone - and rather quickly. I noticed José's brow furrow. He held his tongue, though. Two minutes later Raymond disconnected from the phone.

"Sorry. Business stuff from back home."

"How long have you been married?" I asked him.

"Married?" Raymond asked, raising his eyebrows.

"How'd you pick that up?" asked José.

"He normally wears a silicone ring, I believe," I said to José. "He has a light tan line. If he wore a traditional silver, platinum, or gold ring, he'd have more of a depression on his ring finger."

José turned to Raymond. “My associate here hit it right on the nose. You are fucking married. Why wouldn’t you mention that?”

“What makes you think I am married?” he said, trying to deflect.

“I served six years in the United States Marine Corps. Honorable discharge. A great fucking time.”

“How is that relevant to marriage?”

“Oh, it isn’t,” José angrily said. “My two years in motherfucking France are relevant, though. You were just talking to your fucking wife! You told her that your business speculations in Chicago were troublesome but that you’d be back soon. What the hell kind of shit are you trying to pull?” José yelled.

Raymond’s face fell. I pushed my chair back and moved to get up.

“A wife that doesn’t know why you are traveling, or that you might have birthed a child out of wedlock is trouble. The fact that you aren’t being forthcoming is trouble. I’ll not have a part in sending Charity to a potentially dangerous situation.”

I then got up. José got up, too.

“You are a fucking liar!” José yelled at Raymond. “I asked you if you were married or involved with anyone else and you said no!”

“That is not relevant or admissible in a court of law when trying to determine paternal rights.”

"You are in my motherfucking court!" José said as he threw his arms up in the air. "I got the goods. Marta's got the goods. Until you fucking own up to what you have going on up in Canada, don't fucking call me."

"Please. I am sorry. Can we sit down and talk about this?"

I shook my head. "No. You get your stories and your priorities straight, Mr. Danskin. When Mr. Villanueva - who is an honest, good man - tells me you are good, then I will be more forthcoming with what I know. Goodbye."

With that, I allowed José to escort me from the restaurant. Outside, he cussed a storm for three minutes before falling into silence.

"You were right. That was awesome food," I said to him.

José laughed. "Isn't it? Shit," he said as he shook his hands. "I fucking hate liars."

For a few moments, I considered my father's plight. "People don't always lie out of malice. They do it to protect themselves and others."

"Not to me. I ain't getting paid for this shit. I put in days of work to do the right thing and this motherfucker lies?"

I looked at the restaurant, but I could not see inside.

"Raymond Danskin came down from Canada. Took time off work and paid money to get here and stay here. That's not nothing."

José shook his head again. "Nah, man. He's got to do better than that if he wants to know what I know."

I nodded and then looked at my watch. "I have somewhere else I need to be. Go ahead and buzz me again if Raymond Danskin is ready to be upfront about his situation."

"Yeah. Thanks for coming out. Let me know if you want to get a drink sometime or something."

I laughed out loud, but not in a mocking way. "I'm not interested in that. Take care, José."

"You, too, Marta."

And with that, I headed to my car. Within my vehicle, I stopped the recorder and then looked out at the bar. José was gone, but Raymond Danskin was at the entrance, looking left and right.

He spotted me in the parking lot and came my way. I reached for my pepper spray and allowed him to approach me.

"Hey. You don't approach a single woman in a car in Chicago. It's creepy and scary."

Raymond blushed. "You shouldn't do that anywhere. But I get it. I'm sorry," he said as he stopped short of my car.

"What do you want?"

"My daughter. I want to confirm that she's mine. If she is, I take her home with me and give her the life she deserves."

I stared at him a bit. "Why do you want her?"

"Because my family is big on family. Because I hate hearing that her short life has been so scary."

I shook my head. "It hasn't been scary - not up until now."

"Why?" Raymond asked, panic filling his tone.

I tilted my head. "I have to protect her. Even from you. You have a situation back home that you lied about."

"I am going to get that cleared up. Today. I promise. Could you please give me a lead on Charity?"

I shook my head. "No. You have to go through José. He's the one that's good at vetting people."

"What do you do?"

I shook my head. "That's not your concern. What you should do is go home and talk to your wife. You are married - right?"

Raymond nodded. "I am. One year now. She's from Quebec."

"Go home and let your wife know what you've learned. If it's still a secret, she can't be too mad - not if you tell her now. Also, if she's not going to be a good fit for your daughter and your life as a father, you probably need to cut your wife loose."

In answer, Raymond sunk to the pavement, covering his eyes with his hands.

"I don't know what she's going to do."

I put my window down and looked at where Raymond had taken a seat on the ground.

"Give your wife a chance. Make your decision after you've spoken to her and given her time to process what you'll tell her." I thought about things for a while longer. "Don't take too long, though. There are other good people out there who would love to give Charity a permanent home. If the Chicago courts decide that a Chicago family will give her a good life, I don't know that you will be able to reverse that decision."

Raymond shot up, then. "I can't have that. No, Ma'am."

"Go home, Mr. Danskin. Talk to your wife and your lawyer. Once you are in the clear with José, I will tell your lawyer what I know. Then prepare for a fight." I glanced at his hands and the way he stood. "You look like you are good in a fight. I think that will be of help."

"What do you do?" he asked of me.

"I have to go," I said instead.

Thinking about it, I handed him a business card that only had an email address on it.

"If you do things right and José is still pissed, reach me through this email."

"You got a number?"

"I'm not giving you that. Give my email address to your lawyer, should José not acknowledge your attempts to get on the straight and narrow. Goodbye, Mr. Danskin."

With that, I drove away from the sad father.

"Oh, Angie," I said as I sighed. "What am I going to do?"

Chapter Fifteen

I did what I typically did when I faced a moral dilemma or a professional one.

"*Aha, aha, perate un momento*," said my older brother.

"I thought we were past this," I said in answer.

"Can I finish gassing up my fucking car?"

"Why are you answering your cell phone while you are gassing up your car? Do you want to get lit on fire?"

"That shit was debunked."

"Oh, okay. We can put that on your epitaph: 'Rafael Morales - The Mean Streets of Southie Didn't Kill Him, and Neither Did Puerto Rican Gun Runners, Nor His Dramatic Mother. He Caught Fire While Gassing Up His Vehicle Because That Quote-Unquote 'Shit Was Debunked.'"

A dial tone was Rafy's reply, which was fair. I groaned and pulled over, waiting for him to call back. A couple of minutes later, he called back.

"You had that coming," Rafy said by way of a greeting.

"I'm looking out for you."

"You are looking out for your smart mouth."

I sighed. "That's fair. Hey. Is Dad giving a hand?"

"Yeah. He's helping with the boys and going on about how much fun he had in Chicago."

"Well, he charmed folks. That's for sure," I replied.

"He learned to perform from the best."

"Feds," I said.

"Pigs," said my brother.

We laughed, which was fun.

"Rafy; I am facing a moral dilemma."

"Lay it on me. I'm stuck in fucking traffic anyway."

So, I did. I told him everything – from Angie going to foster parent training to José Villanueva finding Raymond Danskin and up to meeting Raymond Danskin.

"Fuck. Man. This is novela-level shit."

"I know. Angie is like my best friend, but…Charity is a baby. Raymond Danskin might be her father – a man who traveled to a different country to get his daughter and give her a good life."

"*If* he's her father," Rafy qualified.

"He's willing to do the works – DNA tests, background checks, and he's already hired a lawyer."

"Damn."

"What do you think is right?" I asked.

"For whom?"

"For the smallest of victims. Charity."

"The baby's father is best. Her family – if they are good people. Angie might be nice, but she's a single woman. What if something happens to Angie?"

"Charity's back in the system," I answered. "What's the best thing for Angie?"

"She needs her friend to tell her the truth. You are going to hurt her feelings and piss her off. But you don't need to say anything yet. Not until this Raymond Danskin's stuff comes back."

"True."

"Hey. I got to go. But thanks for the drama. Keep me posted, okay?"

"Will do."

That evening, I got an email from Raymond Danskin. He let me know that he'd hired a local lawyer and that he'd spoken to his wife. He asked that I call him.

Cussing, I called José first.

"Why'd that fucker go to you first?"

"Because you scared the Canadian."

"Not the first time that's happened."

"He's offered to do a three-way call with me, him, and his wife," I said.

"Make it a group call with me."

"Alright. Be ready in about fifteen minutes."

Five minutes before I was due to call Raymond, Kevin walked in. I sighed.

“Listen: I am about to go into a group call. You can listen in, but you cannot say anything. Do you understand?”

“Marta,” Kevin groaned as he hung up his jacket and locked the front door. “What now?”

“Deal or no deal?” I asked. “Are you in or are you out?”

“I’m in. Shit. Let me get a beer first.”

So, he was pissed, but then got a beer and sat at the table. After arranging my mini-recorder, my notepad, and my pen, I called José.

“Hey hot stuff,” José said.

Kevin’s eyes widened and he was about to speak. I hushed him with a finger.

“What did I tell you about talking to me like that?”

“You haven’t told me if you have a man.”

“Not sharing that. I’ve got other stuff to do. You ready to get into this?”

“Fuck yes. I’m going to make that Canadian fucker cry.”

Kevin stared at me with wide eyes. I ignored him.

“Okay. Hold on; I am going to conference call him.”

I added Raymond Danskin’s number to the conference call and called him.

“Hello. This is Raymond. Is this you, Marta?”

"Yes, Raymond. José is here."

"Oh. Okay. Good. Hello, Mr. Villanueva."

"What did I tell you about going to my associate first, Raymond?"

"She's nicer than you, Mr. Villanueva."

Kevin looked like he was about to speak.

"We need to get on with this," I said. "Do you have your wife there, Raymond?"

"Yes. Her name is Marie."

"Hello, I am Marie Danskin," said a lightly-accented voice.

I let out a breath.

"What do you know about Cassidy Russo, Mrs. Danskin?"

"I've learned that my husband has been lying to me for two weeks! I am very angry with him."

I nodded.

"Pissed off wife. Works for me," said José.

"I've hired a Chicago-based lawyer, Marta," Raymond said. "I am ready to do whatever I need to to get my daughter home with me – DNA tests, the works."

"I am ready for this, too," said Marie.

"Aren't you pissed, Mrs. Danskin?" Asked José. "Your husband will be bringing another woman's child home."

"My husband does not know this child. We will meet her together. And she is an innocent. What kind of person would have anger towards an orphaned child?"

"Alright, Marta," José said to me. "Do you want to share information?"

I looked at Kevin, who shook his head. He pointed at the pad where he'd written something.

"No. Not until those DNA tests are done. You need to go through DCFS. That's-"

"That is the Department of Children and Family Services in Chicago. I know this," interjected Marie Danskin. "Our lawyer told us this. This is fair. We are strangers. In the meantime, I have called my family's attorney. We will have a home study conducted here in Canada and we will share that with the American authorities."

"That will take time," said Raymond. "I want to meet my daughter."

"Chances are that you are her father," said José. "But until that's proven, we aren't sharing what we know."

"Yes. Raymond will come home and we will prepare with our lawyers," Marie said.

"You want to do this right, Raymond," I said. "That means going through your lawyers, who will go through the state."

"What about the mother – Cassidy? What if she fights this?" asked Marie.

I looked at Kevin, who shrugged.

"You'll want to investigate her, I imagine," I said to Raymond.

"Do you know her, Marta?" asked Raymond.

Kevin shook his head. He then wrote two words on the pad. They made me mad, but they were true.

"You are going to want to hire a private investigator, but talk to your lawyer first," I said as I sighed.

"Will you share information with the investigator?" asked Marie.

I looked at Kevin, who nodded.

"Yes. I will."

"Well, Raymond. I'm glad you came clean with your wife," said José.

"I'm sorry I wasn't forthcoming sooner. To everyone."

"Next time Raymond comes to Chicago, I will be there," said Marie.

"Not my circus, not my monkeys," said José.

"Alright. I'm hanging up," I said.

Kevin pointed at something he'd scrawled on a pad.

"Before I go – Raymond? Don't get a hold of me again. Go through your attorney first. I'll decide if I need to get my attorney involved."

"I understand," he said as he sighed.

With that, I disconnected the call with Raymond and Marie.

"You there?" I asked José.

"Yeah. Why didn't you offer to investigate Cassidy?"

"Because she is involved with some *bad* dudes," I enunciated. "I won't touch her again – not with a ten-foot pole."

"Are you going to share all you know with an investigator?"

I shook my head. "No. All they need to know is how to find Cassidy. Everything else is up to them."

I looked at Kevin, who was staring at me. "Gotta go, José. If I hear something, I'll call you."

"Thanks, Marta. You got plans tonight?"

In answer, I hung up. Exhausted, I slumped into my chair.

"This is novela-level shit, Marta," Kevin said.

"I just want to go to bed. Can we go to bed?"

"No argument from me," was my boyfriend's answer.

The next morning, Kevin talked about what had gone on the night before.

"This is what you do," he said as he shaved his face. "Carry on with life as normal. Tell no one what's going on."

"But what about Angie? She's my friend."

Kevin shook his head. “No. Not even her. If she gets wind of Raymond Danskin looking for his daughter, she might do something stupid and desperate – something she will regret.”

“But what if she’s reasonable? What if she understands that she’s fighting a losing battle? What if she wants a friend?”

Kevin shrugged. “I gave you my advice. And…truth be told, you aren’t beholden to anyone, as you haven’t been hired on this case. However, what if she tries to get canny? What if Angie tries to look up Cassidy?”

I sighed but said nothing by way of answer to that. “I’ll think on it.”

Kevin had to work late that evening, so I met up with Angie for drinks.

“How’s the foster parent training going?”

Angie nodded. “Great. I’m nearly done. How’s your case going – the one with the daughter looking for her dad?”

I nodded. “Done, thank God.” I stared at Angie for a bit. “Angie?”

“What?”

“What if you can’t get Charity?”

“How do you mean?”

“What if she gets adopted by someone else?”

“That would suck. I want this. I want her.”

I nodded. “What if her dad found out about her?”

"Not happening. Cassidy got knocked up in Canada."

"I know, but things happen. You want this and I would feel heartbroken if this didn't happen for you."

Angie reached over and patted my hand. "Your concern is sweet, Marta, but I'm good."

Even though I wanted to say more – to warn my friend – the words dried up in my throat. Would I have to go to confession over it? Would a priest absolve me of the guilt I felt towards my friend? Would he appreciate the duty I felt to a child and her father?

Why was everything so messy? Why was everything so dramatic?

"Hey. How's the boyfriend?" Angie said, thankfully interrupting my sad thoughts.

I sighed. "Good. Kevin was feeling the heat over some cases he was trying to close, but I think that's lightened up. He's going on vacation soon, so I hope that will bring some relief."

"Oh! How fun for him. Where are you guys going?"

I smiled. "I'm not going. And it's not a fun vacation. He's going to Ireland with his parents to see his uncle, who is on his way out."

"Were you not invited?"

I shook my head and sipped wine. "No, but I'm alright with that."

"Really?" Angie said, looking very interested. "Why?"

I thought on an answer for a moment or two. "Because I don't want to go to Ireland with his parents. Because I don't want to meet extended family members as Kevin's girlfriend. I want to meet them when I'm his wife."

"Skipping the fiancé part?"

"Yep," I said as I reached for a nacho chip.

Angie nodded. "How does your dad like Kevin?"

I smiled. "Dad likes him. Kevin's charming and he's a cop. That has a built-in charm of its own."

"Cops get away with a lot of stuff," Angie said as she sighed.

I stared at my friend for a moment. "Hey. You okay?"

Angie shrugged. "I don't know. I guess that I'm scared that things won't work out with adopting Charity."

My chip dried in my mouth.

"What do you think, Marta?" Angie asked.

I thought for a moment before answering. "I think it won't be easy – not at all. I think you have to get ready for a fight."

Angie's brow furrowed. "What do you know?"

"About what?"

My answer was cowardly, and I knew it. I was trying to think up something to say when someone at the table next to us stood up – and crashed into our own.

"Oh, wow!" I exclaimed as I quickly shoved my chair back.

Angie was okay, but looking similarly shocked. Quickly, I crouched down and touched the shoulder of the man who'd passed out on our now-broken table.

"Hey, Sir. Are you okay?" I asked.

The man's companions laughed and pulled the guy up.

"He's okay, ma'am. He gets into his drinks sometimes," said a female at their table.

"Okay. Glad he's okay. My mood's ruined now, though," Angie said as she reached for her purse.

"Me too," I muttered.

After trying to settle our tab (the guys on the table next to us insisted on covering it), we got up and left.

"Are we getting older, or are these haunts getting filled with younger folks?" I asked Angie.

"Both. But it's probably time to call it a night. Text me when you get home, okay?"

"Sure," I said as I hugged her.

After that, I headed home.

"I tried to tell Angie," I said to Kevin. He was in the shower and I was using the mirror while taking my makeup off.

"What?" Kevin asked.

"I tried to tell Angie to not get her hopes up."

Kevin groaned and turned the showerhead off. "Marta; I told you not to tell her anything."

"I didn't. Not really. I just kind of told her to prepare to have to fight for Charity."

Kevin opened the shower curtain and stared at me. "I guess that's reasonable."

"Yeah," I said as I passed him a towel.

Kevin kept staring at me as he dried off. "I feel bad for you. No matter what, you are going to end up being the bad guy. Bad because you didn't warn Angie, and bad because you turned José Villanueva onto finding Charity's father."

"I didn't try to do that. Also, I can't believe how cunning an investigator he is. I think he's better than me, Kevin."

"That's just great. My girlfriend is a better detective than I, and a former marine and landscaper has us both beat."

I laughed.

"How's that funny?"

"I don't know. I guess it will be up to a landscaper and a maid to clean up Chicago's rough streets."

"Less funny, Marta!"

I laughed, and then he did, too.

That Sunday, Kevin and I went to his condo to meet up with his parents, who would be having lunch with us there.

"You didn't mention what you'd be cooking," I said to Kevin as I opened the glass doors in the living room that led to the balcony. His place smelled musty.

"Because I'm not cooking," Kevin said as he opened his fridge and tossed stuff into a trash can.

I turned to face him. "I can't cook. I don't have anything to cook! I don't have ideas or time to panic over cooking for your parents!"

"Relax," Kevin said as he rolled his eyes. "I got catered stuff. It'll be delivered here soon."

I let out a breath of relief.

"Cool. Thank God."

Soon, we were setting up barbequed ribs and chicken on the countertop in the kitchen. Kevin opened some beers for us and put some music on.

"This is nice," I said as I smiled at him.

"Very," he said as he leaned over to give me a quick kiss.

Soon, we were at the table with Doctor and Mrs. Connelly. The catered food made for a good lunch.

"Marta? You won't have to drive us to the airport," said Alice. "Kevin Senior and I will hire a car and will come here to pick up Kevin."

"I won't be here," said Kevin to his mother.

"Oh. Where will you be?" asked Dr. Connelly.

"At Marta's. I stay there now."

Alice set her cutlery down and stared at Kevin. "You went to confession this morning," she reproved.

I blushed and set my eyes on my lap.

"I did," said Kevin as he sighed. "And I won't discuss anything else about it, either. Have some more potato salad," Kevin said as he dumped a huge spoonful of the yellow taters onto Mrs. Connelly's plate.

Thankfully, my phone rang – my sleuther one.

"Uh oh," I muttered.

"Not only am I not a fan of your bat phone ringing right now, but your 'uh-oh' scares me, too," said Kevin.

"Bat phone?" asked Dr. Connelly.

"She has a special phone for her unlicensed investigative work. You can imagine how that makes me feel."

"It's José Villanueva," I said as I groaned.

"Sweet Lord Almighty!" Kevin said. "Take the call, but put it on speaker. "Mom; Dad. You HAVE to shut up. Say NOTHING about what you are about to hear."

Dr. Connelly smiled as he sat back and nodded. Even Mrs. Connelly looked excited.

"Hey, pretty lady. When are you going to go out with me?" said José.

I groaned and shook my head. "Tell me something relevant this Sunday morning or I am going to hang up in your face."

"You got a man, don't you?"

So, I hung up on him.

"This is quite odd," said Dr. Connelly.

"But intriguing," said Diane.

My phone rang again.

"Hang onto your hats," Kevin said. "This will be a roller coaster ride."

I took a call and seethed. "What, José?"

"Alright. I get it. You have a serious thing going on. I'm calling you with a Danskin baby update."

"Oh, my goodness. Oh wow. Are you serious?"

"Damn fucking straight. That geeky Canuck is throwing himself a daddy shower with the help of his Frog wife."

I got up and paced. "Wow. Oh wow. Poor French-Canadian Marie. Also, you are going to have to give me a minute to absorb this."

José laughed out loud. "It's good news – don't you think?"

"That is the aim. But…how did the DNA tests come back so quickly? It's only been five days!"

"Turns out that Charity's DNA was in the system. Raymond's wife Marie comes from money. She paid to have the DNA tests expedited. Charity Russo is now Charity Danskin," José said, gravity filling his voice. "Raymond and Marie are coming to Chicago next week and are not leaving until Raymond gets his little girl back."

"But what about the suitability study?"

"Oh, Marie wasn't busting our balls. She fucking got that shit done. Their Toronto and Chicago lawyers have the DNA tests and the suitability tests in their hands. Fuck.

They even had background checks done. They left no stone unturned."

Dr. and Mrs. Connelly looked intrigued.

"José? What do you think is next?"

"Oh, it's already happened. Marie Danskin hired a private investigator to find Cassidy Russo. That investigator will probably be knocking on your door soon, Marta."

"Sweet Lord almighty," I muttered.

"Marta. I know that you are an unlicensed P.I. and that you've got shit to hide. You are going to want to be careful around the investigator Marie hires. Marie's loaded, so she probably hired the best," Jose advised.

"Aren't you worried?" I asked José.

"Fuck no. Let them come. I ain't got shit to hide. Also, I think this is for the best. Marie is acting like a mother already – far more than fucking good-time girl Cassidy ever was. Not even with her ma on her fucking deathbed and the state taking her daughter did Cassidy fucking grow up. Now Charity has family in Canada fighting to get her? This feels right, Marta."

"Thanks for the heads-up, José. I got to go."

I then hung up. Dr. Connelly and Mrs. Connelly stared at me.

"Kevin?"

"Yeah, baby girl," Kevin said as he rubbed my back.

"Another beer, please?"

"Coming right up," Kevin said as he stood up.

Dr. Connelly was staring at me.

"I won't divulge details about my investigations," I said by way of apology.

"Your client's dead, Marta. That doesn't apply anymore," Kevin called out from the kitchen.

I took my beer from Kevin and took a long swig of it. I then thought about Cassidy and her dangerous boyfriend. I thought about how Cassidy stole money to give to the nurse tending to Cassidy's mother Greta.

Cassidy had been a good-time girl, but now she was a woman who did whatever she had to to protect her daughter. "Cassidy did what she had to do. I fear that this investigator is going to uncover things better left in the dark."

"That comes up a lot more than you think it would," said Mrs. Connelly.

"True story," Kevin said as he leaned back in his chair.

"How do I handle a private investigator, Kevin?"

"Fuck. Chances are I'll be in Ireland when they come calling."

"Divulge as little as possible," said Mrs. Connelly.

I sighed. "Nothing is more obvious than a person hiding something, Diane. My caginess will be a red flag."

"She's good," said to his mother by way of explanation.

"How about this? Right here, right now: tell us what you don't want to come out. We'll brainstorm ways for you to avoid telling what it is you want to keep secret." Said Dr. Connelly.

"Great. A workshop on deceit, held by my evil mastermind family," said Kevin.

Mrs. Connelly laughed out loud. "You are enjoying this."

Kevin half-smiled. "Maybe."

I nodded. "Okay. Good. Yes," I stammered. "Okay. What cannot come out is that Cassidy *is* a good mom. What must be believed is that she is a good-time girl who wants no responsibilities. She needs to remain unfound for as long as possible."

"That is so intriguing," said Mrs. Connelly. "Can't you share a bit more?"

I shook my head no. "I can't."

"We need to think end results, then," said Dr. Connelly. "The best solution is that Charity…Danskin goes to her father's home in Canada. That means that Cassidy is deemed an unfit mother, which should not be a mystery to anyone. Am I right?"

"Can they find her?" asked Mrs. Danskin. "How did you find her?"

I sighed. "It took a lot of work. That's how I met José Villanueva."

"A private investigator will probably take longer than you, but he'll probably find Cassidy," said Kevin. "Especially now that Greta Russo has passed away."

"Greta was Cassidy's mom," I said to Kevin's parents. "Cancer took her about three months ago. She was the one who was acting as Charity's guardian."

"Why would the Danksins come to you for answers, Marta?" asked Dr. Connelly.

"Because I found Cassidy. I talked to her – on the phone and in person."

"You are forgetting the one person who can derail all of this, Marta."

"Who?" asked Dr. Connelly.

"Marta's best friend – Angela Bonacci."

"Okay. How does she fit in?" asked Mrs. Connelly.

Five minutes later held them apprised.

"Wow. This is soap-opera-level drama, Marta," said Dr. Connelly.

"That's not even the fourth time she's heard that, Dad," said Kevin.

Back at my apartment that night, Kevin checked the windows – for a third time.

"I'll be fine, Kevin."

"I don't want to go to Ireland, Marta," he muttered.

I shrugged. "I get it. But everything will be okay over here. And you should get away for a bit."

"You trying to shove me out?" he asked as he pulled me close.

I shook my head. "No. But I know that a continent and an ocean's distance from work might get rid of some of your stress."

"Yeah. Probably. I'll get shitty with my cousins while I eat a lot of bland food."

I turned around in his arms. "Will any Irish girls try to hit on you?"

"Definitely," Kevin teased.

I sighed. "Great."

"I know what I have at home," Kevin said as he kissed my forehead.

Early the next morning, I pouted as I looked out the apartment window and watched Kevin enter a town car bound for the airport.

Seconds later, I felt my phone buzz.

"*Go back to bed*," was the text Kevin sent to me.

Smiling, I did just that.

Chapter Sixteen

Two days later held me counting the days until Kevin's return – two days. Cleaning kept me busy, as did Ana Luz – the protagonist of the sappy novela my mom had turned me onto.

Surprisingly, it was just me and my dad watching the novela. When my dad and I revealed the truth about Ana Luz's activities, Rafy's excitement expired. My mom was still a fan, but her church's choir began practicing every day – during the time the novela came on. (Dad recorded it on a VHS tape for her).

I had just left Barney's Haberdashery and was on my way home, trying to hurry up and get to my TV when someone began walking next to me. Quickly, I pulled my stun gun from my pocket and pointed it at the short man walking next to me.

"Holy Shit, Lady," the man said as he laughed. "Please, don't pull that trigger. I've been tased before and it fucking sucks."

I stared at the guy and figured out who he was – a private investigator. He looked average, wearing khaki pants and a gray windbreaker. He wore clumsy sunglasses that hid his eyes and a good bit of his nose. The pockets of his jacket were heavy, and I knew that he was packing heat – and probably a mini-recorder, too. Shit. If José was right about Marie Danskin's deep pockets, this guy was probably the best money could buy. I had to be careful.

"I am not putting my taser down!" I loudly said. "Who the hell do you think you are, coming up on a woman like this in a town like this?"

Passersby started to slow down and stare. The investigator guy didn't like that.

"Look. My name's Carl Neal. I only want to talk."

"I don't give a shit!" I loudly said. "Just because you gave me your name does not mean that you aren't dangerous."

"I only want to talk," he calmly said.

I shook my head. "No. You are creepy. Stay away from me."

With that, I ran to my car and turned it on. I then joined traffic, going somewhere that was decidedly *not* home.

Not home turned out to be Kevin's condo, which he'd given me the keys to. The doorman greeted me by name, which was great.

I didn't have any of my personal belongings there. After texting my dad, I showered and put on some sweats that Kevin had. They smelled musty. Frowning, I took them off and tossed them into a hamper – which was full.

"Are you kidding me right now?" I whined.

So, wearing nothing but a towel, I did Kevin's laundry.

"You had better put a ring on me," I said to the empty apartment.

After dressing in clean, dry clothing, I ordered Chinese food and watched TV from the comfort of Kevin's living room.

"Wow. This is cozy," I said as I sunk into the couch.

I was dozing off when my phone rang. I didn't recognize the number, so I let it go to voice mail. When I played the message back, I discovered that it was Carl Neal – the investigator.

I looked at Kevin's laptop, which sat on his kitchen counter. Thinking smart, I knew not to look up Carl Neal on the internet. So, I did something else.

"You are calling me from your bat phone," Kevin said in answer. "What's going on?"

"Do you know a Carl Neal?"

I then heard laughing and music in the background. It was probably stereotypical, but I mentally placed Kevin in a pub. Probably surrounded by other redheads.

"Carl Neal? Who is that?" he asked, sounding a lot more alert.

I sighed. "I think he's a private investigator."

"Damn it to hell, Marta. Shit. I knew this shit was going to happen just as soon as I left. Fuck!"

"Hey. Hey! It's okay!" I placated.

"He probably followed you home, Marta, and we still haven't gotten that surveillance system installed. Shit."

"It doesn't make sense to purchase a security system when I am about to be on the market for a new home. Also, I didn't go home."

"Then where are you?"

"At your place. Your doorman won't let the private investigator in, and he'll have no idea where I'd be."

"Oh. That's good thinking."

"How do you have so much dirty laundry?"

Kevin laughed. "Do you mind getting to that for me?"

"I already did," I grumbled. "I needed something to wear."

"Okay. Hold on."

I then heard Kevin order another pint of something. I stereotyped again and made it a Guinness.

"Do you think the investigator has connected me to you?"

"Probably," Kevin said before slurping.

"Would I be that much of a cause of interest?"

"Yes. You told Raymond Danskin – and his wife – that you know how to reach Cassidy. The investigator wants Cassidy, and you are probably his only way to get to her. I bet that Raymond is not understanding why you won't pony up Cassidy's information. He's proven his relationship to Charity."

"So, the more I fight, the more he looks into me?"

"Precisely."

"I don't need that."

"Definitely not."

I sighed. "Okay. I will give him my best number for Cassidy, and I will leave it at that."

"Hey. If this investigator is half as canny as you, he's going to know that you are leaving something out. Just talk to him over the phone."

"He's not trying for that. He wants to talk to me in person."

"Then next time you see him, you go up to him."

"It's not fun being the person being investigated."

Kevin laughed out loud at that.

I went to sleep for the night in Kevin's large bed, where I had dreams about tasers, Irish pubs, and private investigators.

I got up extra early the next morning so that I could dash home and change. Once I was done with that, I quickly made my way to Jane Knight's condo.

"Hey. What have you been into lately?" Asked Jane, who was standing in her kitchen.

I nearly sunk into tears as I told her about the Cassidy/Charity stuff.

"Wow, Marta!" Jane said as she sent a text on her phone. "You are a magnet for chaos."

I groaned instead of answering that.

"You are going to piss off your friend Angie," Jane said.

"I know. I hate that so much."

"But I get it. Family is family. Also, there's no way Angie would ever win custody of Chastity – not if Chastity's biological father didn't know of her, now wants her, and is throwing all sorts of money into getting her back."

"Should I warn Angie?"

"Why didn't you warn her?"

I blushed. "I tried, but…I chickened out."

"You didn't want her to know that you are on Team Dad."

Instead of answering, I hung my head in shame.

I carried on with the day's cleanings.

When Carl Neal confronted me outside of Jamie's Pawnshop, I stopped for him.

"What do you want?" I tiredly asked.

Carl Neal shrugged. "Can I buy you a coffee?"

I could go for a coffee.

"Not until you tell me who you are and what you want."

"Okay. I'm a private investigator."

I sighed and nodded. "Does this have anything to do with Cassidy Russo?"

Carl smiled. “It has everything to do with that.”

“Fine. Then you can buy me a coffee – and a donut.”

Carl laughed out loud. I didn’t.

We stopped at a small café I wasn’t familiar with. The flavor of the donut recommended by Carl surprised me.

“Wow. This packs a kick,” I said as I looked at the spicy chocolate donut.

Carl laughed out loud. “I know. I love surprising folks with that.”

“Good one. Now. I have other clients to get to today. Can you ask your questions?”

Carl nodded and then grabbed a notepad and a tape recorder. I wondered if he knew that I knew that he was already filming me.

“Do I have your permission to record this?”

I was going to say yes, but then I remembered about Cassidy’s sketchy boyfriend.

“You do not. I do not consent to being recorded in any manner – audio or video.”

Carl’s face fell. Still, he reached for something in his pocket and hit a button.

“Why don’t you want to be recorded?”

“Because I said no. Now. Ask your questions.”

“Did your detective boyfriend teach you that stuff?”

"No. Law and Order reruns did. Ask your questions, Carl."

Carl laughed. "Okay. How can I reach Cassidy Russo?"

I pulled out my cell phone. "Write this number down."

Quickly, he did.

"Is there anything else I should know?"

I sighed. "I don't know, Carl. Do you want a weather forecast? Your horoscope? The farm report?"

Carl laughed again. "I like you, Marta. Okay. I will ask you a question. Why are you showing resistance to my questions?"

"Because you are a private investigator. It's your job to be nosy and my job to be guarded."

"Fair enough. What else should I know about Cassidy Russo?"

I sighed. "That she's a good girl, deep down inside. She loved her mother and she loved her daughter."

"Bad way of showing it."

I shrugged. "I know."

"Do you think she'd resist Raymond Danskin's attempts to get custody of his daughter?"

I sighed. "I would hope not. It seems like Raymond and his wife are trying to do right by Charity."

"Will I find Cassidy at this number?" Raymond said as he pointed at the number on the pad.

I chuckled. "Cassidy is squirrely. She's good at not being found if she doesn't want to be found."

"I need to find her, Marta."

I nodded. "Honest to God, I hope you do."

"So, how do you like cleaning, Marta?"

With that, I grabbed my purse and my jacket.

"Hey. Where are you going?" Carl asked as he laughed. "We were getting to know each other."

"Thank you for the coffee, Carl. Best of luck to you and the Danskin family."

That evening, I watched the novela with my dad. After that, I cleaned the heck out of my apartment. Kevin was coming home the following day. I knew he probably wouldn't notice, but I still put forth the effort.

My phone rang late in the night. I braced myself and took the call.

"Did you know?" asked Angie.

"Know about what?"

"Don't be cagey with me, Marta! You are supposed to be my friend!" she yelled into the phone.

"Okay, okay," I said as I sat up in my bed. "I am not going to keep anything from you."

"But you did that."

"Tell me what you know and I will fill in the rest of the blanks."

"Cassidy's dad has been found and he wants her back."

I sighed. "That is true."

"Why didn't you tell me? Were you hired by them?"

"I didn't find Raymond. I didn't even *try* that," I said, defense filling my tone of voice.

"Then who did?"

I sighed. "Another investigator I know."

"Who? Carl Neal?"

I shook my head. "No. Someone else."

"Who?"

"No one you know." Great. I was protecting Jose Villanueva, who probably needed no protection.

"Great. More secrets, Marta! What kind of friend are you?"

"The other investigator called to let me know what he'd done, how he'd done it, and that Raymond Danskin was in town."

"How long have you known?"

I sighed. "About two weeks."

"You tried to tell me – didn't you?"

I swallowed at tears. "I did."

"Why couldn't you come out and say it?"

"Because I was worried about what you might do. I know that Charity's foster parents have been letting you visit with her. I worried that you might try to take her or something."

"Oh, wow. You know what? No. I don't believe that. You know I'm not a psychopath."

I got up and paced my apartment, grateful that my windows were closed, being that all I wore was a tank top and panties.

"I betrayed your trust, Angie."

"You know what? Fuck that. It sounds like you knew what you were doing. You made a choice and you didn't pick me."

I sighed. "Okay. Someone hired me."

"Who? You just said no one hired you!"

"Cassidy. And Greta, by default."

"What the fuck are you talking about? You just said that no one hired you."

"The night I spoke to Cassidy a few months back? Cassidy asked me to take cash – thousands of dollars – to Greta so that Greta could take care of Charity. Cassidy is keeping her distance from Charity to keep Charity away from Cassidy's very dangerous boyfriend," I carefully said. "If Charity is in another country with her father, Charity is harder to get to. Greta wanted a safe place for Charity. That is not Chicago. It is not close to Cassidy."

"No, Marta. No," Angie said, but I could tell that her arguments were starting to leave her.

"I don't think that the investigator Carl Neal is going to find Cassidy. I'm a better investigator than Carl, and I don't think I could find her again. She's hiding, and it's for the best. Charity in another country is for the best."

Angie was crying on the phone, but her sobs weren't loud.

"You are right, Angie. I did you wrong. I should have trusted you, but I let my ideals get in the way. If you want to cuss me out and hang up on me, I will accept that. And anything else you have to give. Because I am sorry."

"I hate you for this," Angie said.

After that, I heard nothing else.

I was sleeping on the couch with a bedsheet on when I heard the sound of a key opening a lock. Kevin was at the door, and he was smiling.

"It's good to be home," he said.

I laughed.

"Come here!" he demanded.

I did.

Chapter Seventeen

Over the following week, things moved *very* quickly. Raymond and Marie Danskin rented a short-term apartment downtown – with a room for Charity. They were going to throw a "Welcome Back to the Family" party for Charity. I was invited, as was José. Kevin was working, so I asked Angie to accompany me.

"Fuck you," was her answer on the phone.

I called her back anyway and told her that I'd be outside her condo half an hour before the party was due to start.

On the day of the party, I waited outside of Angie's condo. I was surprised when she came to my car, gift in hand.

"I still hate you," Angie whispered to me as she climbed into the passenger side of my car.

I swallowed at a knot in my throat. "That's fair. I bought you a coffee," I said as I pointed to a cup holder.

"You owe me a lot more than that."

"There's a cinnamon roll in the backseat."

Angie laughed. "I hate you," she repeated.

"I understand," was my reply, but I smiled as I said it.

I couldn't help but cry as I saw the grand celebration that Raymond and Marie had thrown for Charity within their rented townhome.

Charity Danskin looked beautiful with her light brown hair and gorgeous blue eyes. Her pink, ruffled dress was adorable. Raymond and Marie could not take their eyes off of her.

Pink streamers adorned the living room and the kitchen. Pink cakes and cupcakes sat on a table. A big "Welcome Home" banner hung from the ceiling.

I dried my eyes as I looked at everything.

"This is wonderful," I said to Marie – a tall blond, model-looking woman. "I hope you are getting this on film."

Marie smiled and dried her eyes. "We are."

Just then, an older woman set a camcorder down. I was astonished when I saw that she had Charity's amazing blue/green eyes.

"Hello. I'm Lisa. Raymond's mom. Charity's grandmother," she said as she beamed.

"What a pleasure it is to meet you," I said to her.

Raymond sat on the floor next to Charity, pushing all sorts of plastic farm animals her way. Charity smiled as she grabbed them and held them to her chest.

Raymond pointed at his chest. "Daddy," he whispered. "I am Daddy."

"You my daddy?" Charity whispered.

Raymond sobbed for a moment. "Yes. I belong to you. I am Charity's daddy."

Charity got up and sat in Raymond's lap before picking up more toys. Raymond gently rested his forehead on the back of Charity's head while he cried silent tears.

José was well-behaved.

"I feel like overdid my gift, Mrs. Danskin," Jose said as he handed a big box to Marie.

Marie smiled and retrieved the box. "What is this?"

"One of my guys paints doll houses for a living. It's a big, massive thing. Don't open it now, though. Wait until she and Raymond are done with the farmhouse."

Marie beamed. "Thank you, José."

Soon, Angie began to talk to Marie. I watched as Marie's expression became serious. Marie grabbed a notepad and a pen and then ushered Angie to the dining table.

"Please. Tell me all you know about the Russo family," Marie begged.

"Marta. Come outside with me," said José.

I had a feeling José had something to show me, so I followed him outside.

José and I walked to the gate of the townhome. He then pulled a cigarette from a box and put it in his mouth.

"You smoke?" I said, as I was shocked.

"No. It's fake," José grumbled. "I haven't smoked for about twenty years now. But I like the feeling of a cigarette in my mouth when I'm stressed."

"Why are you stressed?" I asked him. "This," I said as I pointed to the townhome hosting a party, "is a success that is one hundred percent owed to you. You've just proved that you are the best investigator in Chicago."

José laughed out loud. "Shit. You are making me blush, Marta. Thank you. That means a lot."

"Then why are you nervous?"

José let out a breath. "Because of this."

José pulled a cell phone from his pocket and hit a couple of buttons before hanging it up. Instantly, a cold feeling hit me.

"What did you do?"

"A mom never stops being a mom, Marta. You know this."

Did I ever.

From out of nowhere, the very beautiful but troubled Cassidy Russo walked up the sidewalk. Tears filled my eyes as I watched her walk to the window of the townhouse rented by the Danskins. I walked behind her and looked as Cassidy observed Raymond and Charity put an array of farm animals atop a white leather couch.

"Please, please tell Raymond thank you," Cassidy said as she turned to me and held my hands.

With that, Cassidy pushed something into my left hand and ran away. José and I read it, closed it, and then went back inside the townhome.

"Hey, Raymond," José said as we sat next to him on the couch.

"Hey, you two. I'm getting my little girl used to farm animals here. I get a feeling she hasn't seen many out this way."

José handed a beautifully carved wooden doll to Charity. Charity laughed and held it and then put it on a horse.

I handed Cassidy's letter to Raymond.

"What's this?" he asked. We said nothing. Raymond read it – twice.

"Marie!" He called as he quickly stood up.

Suddenly, his wife was at his side. Marie read the letter and nodded. She then took the letter with her and got on the phone before walking into another room.

"Cassidy was here?" Raymond said.

I nodded. "Yeah."

"Why couldn't she speak to me?"

I shook my head. "Trust me; you don't want that."

"You do not, Mr. Danskin," José gravely seconded.

"It is binding!" Marie called out. "*Nous devons partir. A présent*!"

I turned to Marie, who was hurriedly putting a coat on Charity before putting one on herself.

"What's happening?" questioned Destiny – Charity's foster mother.

"We are taking our daughter and we are going home," Marie announced. "Please; feel free to call your lawyer. Hand them this," Marie said as she presented a photocopy of the letter that Raymond had just shared with her.

"How do I know if this is binding?" asked Destiny as she looked at the sheet of paper that Marie handed her.

Raymond Danskin put on an insulated denim jacket and grabbed his keys, wallet, and something black and metal, which he put in his back pocket.

"Like my wife said," he said, sounding curt. "We are leaving. Call your lawyer. Call the Department of Child Services. I don't quite care. I'm taking my baby home and no one's going to stop me."

I nodded. "Don't take your things," I said to Raymond and Marie. "Leave them here and call someone to get them. We'll linger here and will make it look like the party is still in full swing."

"Yeah," José chimed in. "You are going to want to take the back alleys out of here until you get to Interstate 90. We'll make it look like your party is still going on for a couple more hours."

"Done," said Raymond. "Mom, leave your stuff. Marie, get the baby."

Quickly, I stuffed the plastic animals into a plastic bag, which I then handed to Marie. Marie nodded at me, and while holding Charity, she followed Raymond. The Danskins – all four of them – left the townhome through a back door.

I heard the sound of a large truck turn on and then drive away.

"I don't understand this," said Destiny. "Never mind. I'll call the state."

"Do that," said José.

José then went to the radio, where he blasted a station featuring country songs. He then went to the cake.

"Who wants cake?"

"I'll take some," said Angie. "What was in that letter?" Angie asked me.

I went to the big fridge in the townhome's swanky kitchen and pulled three bottles of beer from it.

"It was a notarized letter from Cassidy Russo, stating that she relinquished all custody and visitation rights of Charity to Raymond and Marie Danskin – effective an hour ago. Another letter in there was a post-it note," I said before having a long swallow of beer.

"What did that say?" asked Destiny.

"It said '*Get out. He knows.*'" Said Jose.

"Who knows what?" Destiny questioned.

"Cassidy's mobster boyfriend learned about Charity," I somberly said.

"Sweet Lord almighty," said Angie.

José walked to the windows and opened the curtains. "A fucking mobster boyfriend. Shit. I bet he has her followed at all times."

"Yeah," I said as I sighed.

I turned to Charity's former foster mother. "If you could leave through the back door, that would be great. You aren't going to want to be here soon."

Destiny left – and in a hurry.

"You should leave, too," I said to Angie.

"Fuck you," Angie snapped at me. "And why didn't you tell me things were this bad?"

I sighed. "Because I hoped they weren't."

"I am no match for a mobster," Angie said with a sigh.

"No one is," said José. "Not even a foul-mouthed Marine like me," José said as he looked out the curtains.

"Marta. We should go," said Angie.

I was in mortal danger. I knew that. Still, I shook my head. "No. I am still under contract with Greta Russo. I will do what I can to see Chastity Russo Danskin to safety."

"Such a fucking cowgirl," Angie said to me as she rolled her eyes.

I laughed, and then she did, too.

Over the next hour, José, Angie, and I laughed and told each other stories about dealing with sketchy people. When the sun went down, José went to the windows and looked outside.

"Three late-model, black cars," he said as he let out a breath. "Could they not be more obvious? Ladies? The bad guys are here."

Fear filled my veins like ice.

"Did we give them enough time to get away?" I asked José.

"I think so," he lightly said.

I said a prayer and then sent a text out. After that, I got up and stared at three cars parked across the street.

"Well, I'm ready for a showdown," José said.

"Are you for real?" said Angie.

"Yeah. Fuck these thugs. They only win if we run scared. I wasn't scared of psychotic Afghans. I sure as fuck ain't scared of gangbangers," José barked.

Just then, José reminded me of Rafy. I smiled.

My smile dropped when I looked out the window. Three large men were making their way across the street.

"Well, shit. One of them is packing and he's crossing the street. Lights, Marta," José said.

Suddenly, I heard police sirens coming from both sides of the road. "No need. The cavalry is here."

José, Angie, and I watched as six cop cars boxed in the three black cars. A boy in blue yelled at the men who nearly made it to the townhome where we were. The cop screamed at one of the armed thugs – telling him to put his hands up. Thankfully, the thug complied with the request.

"Now, the one thing that's scarier than thugs are the Chicago PD. Those motherfuckers will fuck you up and not lose sleep about it."

"Marta?" Angie asked.

"Yeah?"

"Did you call the big bad detective?"

"I sure did."

José looked at me. "Who?"

I kept looking out the window for a red-headed officer. I spotted him and a bald cop walking towards the largest of the three black cars.

"Marta's boyfriend. The police detective," Angie said.

José laughed out loud. "Should have known you'd have a man like that."

I smiled but said nothing to that.

Chapter Eighteen

It was a very exciting end to the evening. My panicked text to Kevin made him panic and call a few cop cars – and for good reason. It turned out that Cassidy's boyfriend was a mobster who knew the right people – up until the moment he and three other guys were found with illegal, high-powered rifles.

Lots of arrests went down. The mayor and the governor called Kevin's captain – congratulating Kevin and the other on-site detective on the high-profile arrests that were made.

José called Raymond's lawyer and learned that the Danskins had made it to Canada safely. I thanked God for that. Raymond's lawyer relayed a message to me and José – that we had friends in Canada – forever.

We were questioned in the precinct that I knew very well. I relayed every iota of knowledge I had of Cassidy Russo, and even the contents of the letter Cassidy had passed onto Raymond and the copy that Charity's foster mother Destiny had taken with her.

"I'm taking my woman home," Kevin said to the captain.

The captain nodded. "Sure thing, Kevin."

"I'll take Angie home," José said to me.

Angie blushed, but I said nothing to that.

We went home to Kevin's condo, which was an interesting choice.

"Marta," he said to me as we made it to his place.

"Yeah," I said as I took my shoes off and set them at the door.

"You are a vector of trouble, woman."

I sighed. "I'm sorry. I made more work for you."

Kevin shrugged. "I don't care about that. This case is clear and cut. Heck, I might even get a promotion out of it. But that's not what I mean. You are kryptonite to bad guys, and that's not a compliment."

"I've made some enemies."

"You have more enemies than I do, Marta. What am I going to have to do here? Fuck! Marry you and take you to Ireland? Have you made any enemies out that way?" He angrily questioned.

I cringed. "I might have said that Bono had short man's disease – in mixed company."

Kevin laughed out loud. "That would make you friends out that way – not the opposite."

"You said you were going to marry me. You can't take that back," I said as I sank onto the couch.

"I never meant to," he said as he yawned. "I just have to put some stuff together first."

"That works for me," I said as I put my head on his shoulder.

I had fallen asleep when I heard him speak again.

"John Carroll," Kevin said.

"Who's that?"

"That's the mobster who got bail to the tune of two million American dollars."

That woke me right up. "Sweet Jesus."

"Yeah. So, that's…Maria Robles, Niels Erickson, Agustin Trujillo's kin, and John Carroll. Let's not forget the FBI. Because they are involved in this case. Oh, and Edna Nazario, too."

Feeling suddenly nauseated, I ran to the bathroom and puked in Kevin's toilet.

"Wow," Kevin called out. "Seriously?"

After brushing my teeth and washing my face, I joined him on the couch.

"Are you okay?" he said as he handed me a glass of water, which I drank.

"Yeah. I had too much beer and cake."

I stared at Kevin for a bit.

"You came when I called."

"I always will."

I hugged him and didn't let him go.

Chapter Nineteen

Kevin was working late, putting in hours to ensure that John Carroll – my latest arch-enemy – would get behind bars and stay there.

"That isn't as funny as you think it is," Dad said to me on the phone. Dad had asked where Kevin was, and I had told him.

"I'm not laughing," I said as I put the phone on speaker.

"You are too cavalier."

I groaned and hit pause on the novela. "Dad. I told you what went down. Every minute, tiny detail."

"I know you did. You were textbook. One hundred percent."

I laughed. "Angie and José have gone on a few dates."

Dad laughed out loud. "I bet she's forgiven you already."

"She has. Angie told me that there was no way that she would have been able to keep Charity away from a mobster."

"You were operating with facts that no one else had, Marta. You are a dangerous good guy."

I laughed. "I like that. Kevin doesn't, though," I said as I sighed. "He worries."

"We all do."

As I left Barney's haberdashery the next day and walked to my car, Carl Neal began to walk next to me.

"I didn't know who you were, Marta," Carl said to me.

"Being that you didn't know me…that tracks," I said.

Carl laughed. "I'm a retired federal agent," he said in a low voice.

"Come on!" I barked. "I can't swing a dead cat and miss one of you cretins. God!" I said as I stomped.

That made Carl laugh out loud – and hard.

"This isn't funny. You have no idea how much of a pain you guys are. God."

"I know, I know. Cops and investigators don't like us."

"No one does," I whispered.

Carl laughed again. "Fuck, Marta. Stop making me laugh. I want to tell you something serious."

"Tell me and leave me alone, you dirty fed."

"I couldn't find Cassidy like you did. I sure as hell couldn't learn who her boyfriend was. You are good at what you do."

"Cleaning?" I hedged.

"Sure. That. Keep at it – and how you are doing it. If you aren't listed, the bad guys will have a harder time finding you."

"Well, it's harder, but not impossible," I said as I sighed.

"Ain't that the truth."

"I got to go. See you, Carl."

With that, I left.

At home that night, I watched the novela with Kevin at my side.

"Where's your dad?" Kevin asked before sipping his beer.

"The twins have a big game. He didn't want to miss it. He's DVRing the show. But it's the series finale."

The show featured a scene so deep that it made me take the bowl of Doritos away from Kevin because he was eating too loud.

"What?" he challenged.

"Hush," I said as I slid closer to the TV.

Ana Luz, the protagonist, was crying as she emptied the safe deposit box of her ex-boyfriend, Ángel Alexis, and his new fiancé, Marielena – Ana Luz's ex-best friend.

"She wished them well," I said out loud. "At their engagement party."

"Why wouldn't she?" asked Kevin.

"Ana Luz shouldn't be crying," I said in explanation. "Ana Luz forgave her boyfriend for leaving her. She wished him well. She shouldn't be this upset."

When Ana Luz got back to her secret apartment, she pulled out a cell phone and dialed a number – and spoke in flawless English the entire time. Spanish captions bounced off the bottom of the TV screen in time with Ana Luz's words.

"*You see,*" said the male voice on the other line. "*They let you down. They always do, and you always come back to me,*" said the voice.

"*No. They wanted to be my friends,*" Ana Luz cried.

"*Maybe they did, but you'll never know. You took their money.*"

"*I'll turn myself in to the police. I'll do it.*"

"*They still won't forgive you,*" said the voice. "*All you will be is a locked-up, friendless woman. All you'll ever be.*"

Ana Luz shook her head. "*I am more than that.*"

"*Are you, though?*"

Ana Luz hung up the phone and stared off into space. "*I'm locked up already. I don't need a prison.* Nadie ama a Ana Luz."

No one loved Ana Luz. It was poignant and tragic.

And then the screen faded to black.

"What? What was that?" Kevin protested.

"Wow. Wow!" I exclaimed.

"That's like…Hitchcock-level stuff," Kevin said. "Who was the guy on the other line?"

I shrugged. "I don't know. I think…we are not meant to learn that. I think that the lesson is…that women make prisons for themselves."

Kevin scoffed. "That is some dramatic bullshit. Give me that remote."

So, I did.

The next evening, though, I watched the finale again – with my mom and dad on the phone and Rafy on his phone.

My family exclaimed and yelled in shock at all of the right times. Mom had the same takeaway that I did.

"We will never see a show like that again!" Mom exclaimed.

"I know," I said as I sighed. "I am sorry that I didn't give Ana Luz the benefit of the doubt."

"Why would you?" Rafy asked. "She was a thief. Sure, a messed-up thief, but a lot of women criminals are fucked up in the head anyway."

Mom and I yelled at Rafy over that. Dad laughed the entire time.

"Women are mysteries," Dad said.

"Changing the subject, I got another call from José Villanueva. He gave me information that explains why Marie Danskin – Charity's new stepmother – is not a mystery."

"Spill," said Rafy.

"Marie Danskin is thirty years old. When she was nineteen, she was diagnosed with uterine cancer. They had to take the whole thing out."

"Poor thing," Mom said.

"Raymond married her – even knowing that Marie could never have kids. Then, a year after they married, they learned that Raymond had a daughter in the American foster care system that he didn't know about. No price was too high to get the little girl in their home. According to José, Marie even quit her job at her family's mineral mining corporation to become a full-time mom to Charity. Raymond's taking time off the family farm operation, too."

Mom sighed. "That is a beautiful ending, Marta. Thank you for sharing that."

Marie wasn't mysterious. Neither was Cassidy, who, according to Kevin, was now missing. Secretly, I wished her the best.

I wasn't mysterious, I thought to myself. I made my wants clear, and people listened. The day prior, Kevin asked for a copy of my birth certificate and my social security card. It was for his insurance policies, he said. I told him that I loved him and he said he knew that.

But my father wasn't wrong regarding the nature of women.

I went to my post office box the next day and found a letter from Melissa Bollinger. It was a heavy envelope – embossed and stuff.

In the privacy of my car, I opened it.

It was a wedding invitation. Melissa Bollinger was marrying a man named Christian Lightfoot in three weeks, and I was invited.

I called Kevin, who was at work, and told him about what I'd received in the mail.

"Wow. Did you want to go to that?" He asked.

I sighed and thought about everything I had going on in my life.

"I…I don't think so. I wish Melissa well, but she's been willingly absent from my life for well over a year now. The invitation might be a courtesy and not an actual request for my presence," I protested.

"I bet it's a real invitation, Marta."

I sighed. "Maybe. But…. I worry that Niels Ericsson might make an appearance."

"A very valid concern, Marta."

Exhausted, I sank on my couch. "I've made too many enemies, Kevin. I can't keep making them. I have to take care of the people who are here for me now. I have a lot of things I want to live for. I can't be the hero. Heroine. You know what I mean."

Kevin was quiet for a while. His breath sounded loud and stuttered.

"Hey, are you okay over there?" I asked.

Kevin took a breath. "Yeah. Yes," he said as he cleared his throat. "I love you so much."

I smiled. "I love you more."

Off the phone, I grabbed the RSVP card and stared at it a bit.

Using a pen, I checked the “no” box and placed the card in the self-addressed-stamped envelope.

“I wish you the best, Amiga,” I said to the sealed envelope.

I then got up and went to my bedroom to read a book – a non-fiction title. I was ready for non-drama.

###

Hello, Reader!

Did you enjoy reading *Marta Gets Soapy* as much as I enjoyed writing it? I hope so.

If you did, would you please leave me a review? I'd love it if you could share your opinion with others – even if you were only okay with my book. (But especially if you loved it.)

Thank you in advance for going to your e-book retailer and telling me your thoughts on *Marta Gets Soapy, Book Five of the Housekeeping Detective Series*.

About the Author

Cyndia Rios-Myers is a Pennsylvania, USA-based writer and essayist who enjoys reading, hiking, Bigfoot videos, good laughs, and long naps. You can keep up with her musings on her Facebook page, on Goodreads, on Instagram, or on X @criosmyers.

Other Titles by Cyndia Rios-Myers

The Housekeeping Detective Series:

Marta Cleans Up: Book One of the Housekeeping Detective Series

Marta Bleaches Everything: Book Two of the Housekeeping Detective Series

Marta Gets Spooked: Book Three of the Housekeeping Detective Series

Marta Gets the Ax: Book Four of the Housekeeping Detective Series

La Serie de la Sirvienta Detective:

La Limpieza de Marta: Libro Uno de la Serie de la Sirvienta Detective

Marta Blanquea Todo: Libro Dos de la Serie de la Sirvienta Detective

Marta Se Asusta: Libro Tres de la Serie de la Sirvienta Detective

Women's Fiction Titles:

Nice Shootin', Tex!

Joppa Park

Horror/Fantasy Titles:

Rescued by the Wolf: Book One of the Wolves

Gifted by the Wolf: Book Two of the Wolves

Mated by the Wolf: Book Three of the Wolves

Condemned by the Wolf: Book Four of the Wolves

Defended by the Wolf: Book Five of the Wolves

Unveiled by the Wolf: Book Six of the Wolves

Razed by the Wolf: Book Seven of the Wolves

The Wolf and the Woman: Jennifer Cleary's Second Chance

Made in the USA
Columbia, SC
09 July 2025